I, CLAWED

Book Two: DOG DAYS

Copyright 2018

The right of Cindy Foley to be identified as the Author of the Work has been asserted by her in accordance with the Copyright, Designs, and Patents Act of 1988.

Apart from any use permitted under US copyright law, this publication may only be reproduced, stored, or transmitted, in any form, or by any means, with prior permission in writing of the publishers, or, in the case of reprographic production, in accordance with the terms of licenses issued by the Copyright Licensing Agency.

All characters in this publication are fictitious and any resemblance to real persons, living or dead, is purely coincidental.

Published by Alix Publishing
Pensacola, Florida

Dedication

This book is dedicated to all the workers, doctors, and volunteers who work at animal shelters.

…especially to Drs. Paul and Jen Sikoski who own Palm Bay Animal Clinic, Coquina Shores Animal Clinic, Clearlake Animal Hospital, and Oakview Animal Hospital, the veterinarians who saved Lily (her story is within these pages.)

Thank you.

Acknowledgments

I want to thank my critique partners, all published authors: Kathryn Flanagan, Peggy Insula, Harry C. Jensen, James R. Nelson, and Gene Vlahovic for the many hours they put into helping me write this story and its prequel *I Clawed; The Renewal.*

You are the best writing partners ever. I could not have finished this novel without your steady influence, consistent instruction, and thoughtful encouragement. Thank you.

I also want to thank my brother, Andy Alix, author, for his expert skill in Microsoft Word.

Mostly I want to thank my cat, Clawed, who hopefully is now a resident of Bling. He was and still is the inspiration behind this story.

Cover and Interior Clip Art: moziru.com

"No, you don't know what it's like
When nothing feels all right
You don't know what it's like
To be like me
To be hurt
To feel lost
To be left out in the dark
To be kicked when you're down
To feel like you've been pushed around
To be on the edge of breaking down
And no one's there to save you
No, you don't know what it's like
Welcome to my life"
      —Simple Plan
      Album: "Still Not Getting any…" (2004)

Chapter 1

In the middle of a blazing hot Florida summer...

... I, Clawed, felt at peace with the world.

I probably should have expected that things could change. One of my flaws—I don't like change. Not many folks do.

For some reason, I was sleeping a lot lately. I had just woken up from an afternoon nap and didn't feel like my usual, bright-eyed and bushy-tailed self.

I'd been having the strangest dream about Gidget who used to live with Sage and Ben and me, key words being, "used to." Gidget and I had been through a lot together, but I hadn't seen her since she became Secretarycat of Bling.

My heart twisted. I missed her. Tabbert told me he'd seen her. Even though I'd searched the house and gardens until I thought my eyes would bug out of my head, I hadn't seen her.

Nothing stirred in the cool air-conditioned house. I needed some fresh air. It was humid and hot as a tin roof, but being outside always helped me feel better.

Not meaning to be unkind about my best friend, Tabbert, a Florida anole, I sort of hoped he wasn't around today. His incessant babble could be annoying at times. I wasn't in the mood for chitchat.

I yawned. Sage and Ben must have gone to the Humane Society thrift store, or … somewhere. I jumped off the back of the couch and checked out my dish.

After gobbling up a smidgeon of crunchies, I slipped through the partially open sliding glass door to the screened-in patio. I nosed around a bit, passed my carpeted cat tower, and jumped through the cat door to go outside.

My eyes steamed over. Yuk. August. Dog days. I considered going back in, but the quiet lull of the day drew me out of the isolated chill of the house.

As quietly as I could and keeping my claws crossed, I kept to the shadows close to the house. I didn't see Tabbert anywhere. I tiptoed around to the side yard, slunk across the well-groomed grass, hurried past the pond where Gidget had disappeared, and headed for the woods. Maybe it would be a bit cooler there.

I entered a clearing in the middle of a dense forest of pines, palms, and oaks, where kids sometimes camped overnight or just hung out for a day. It looked the same as always. Big logs for sitting on surrounded a fire pit ringed with smooth river rocks.

Hoping for a chicken-wing bone or a piece of scorched hot dog, I sniffed the cold ashes. Nothing. Not that I was hungry. I was well-fed. My round belly was a testament to that.

I sat back and gazed around. My studious inspection stopped on the rusty steel shopping cart that usually stood, full of wood, near the fire pit.

The cart had been turned over onto its side. A piece of plywood with a hole in it about as big around as my middle was zip-tied to the top. A cover? For what?

It didn't seem like anyone had been in the clearing for a while.

Ahh. Peace and quiet.

Not.

"Hello there."

I resisted the urge to shake my head. "Hey. What're you doing, Tikky?"

"Not much. Too hot."

"I hear that."

Maybe if I just kept going, he'd get the hint that I didn't feel like company right now. Fat chance. Tikky didn't care much what others thought.

Not that that's always a bad thing. I mean, when we get caught up worrying about what others think, our brains can turn to scrambled eggs.

Sheesh. I was starting to think like Tabbert. I hoped I didn't start babbling like he does. I slipped through the brush and headed toward the citrus grove.

Tikky stayed right on my tail. "What's new at your house?"

The drilling buzz of the summer cicadas cut through my head. I sat, licked my paw, and washed my face. A dragonfly whizzed by. Tikky sat, too.

"Not much," I said.

We sat in the shade of an orange tree.

Tikky and I managed to get along once I'd gotten to know him.

First time we'd met hadn't been so good. He'd tried to take over my yard. Even though he looked a lot bigger than me, I wasn't about to back down. I chased him to the woods. Come to find out he was nothing more than a big orange ball of fluff and huff.

Pretty soon I got used to him coming up on our front porch to get the treats Sage put out for him every day. I wasn't worried about that. I already mentioned I had plenty to eat.

Tikky lived in the woods by his own choice. I suppose it was tough to find food out there sometimes. Hunger can make any of us irritable. By the looks of his round belly, he found enough to eat.

His fluffy, long fur looked matted and dirty. He didn't seem to mind.

Even though it's not everything, it is my educated opinion that appearances are important. I wash daily, wipe my whiskers after every meal, and rub along the back of the couch to keep my black coat looking shiny and sleek. Folks call me a Halloween cat.

I was about to doze off when something thudded against my side. It felt like a huge spit ball.

"Oof." Tabbert bounced off me and fell over backwards. Just as quickly, he was up on his feet again. Eyeing Tikky, he scooted closer to me and clung to my fur. Tabbert would probably never trust that Tikky wouldn't eat him.

Since I became friends with Tabbert, I don't eat lizards anymore. Once I found out that Tabbert could change colors, from green to yellow or gray, even brown, I didn't want to make a mistake and eat someone in his family.

"What's your hurry, reptile?" Tikky asked.

Tabbert straightened his shoulders. His dewlap flared. "How many times do I have to ask you not to call me that? I have a name."

"Whatever." Tikky yawned and looked away.

"You'd better skedaddle," Tabbert said. "There's a big dog chasing me."

The words were no sooner out of his mouth when something crashed through the woods. I made a beeline for the closest tree. I scrambled up the trunk and crouched in the crook of the lowest branch. Tabbert clung to my ear for dear life.

Crazy Tikky darted in another direction, squeezed through the hole in the board covering the shopping cart, and huddled in the corner just as a filthy yellow mongrel barreled into the middle of the clearing and came to a screeching halt.

The dog looked around, shoved his face into the ground, and followed his nose to the base of the tree where Tabbert and I sat. A bark exploded from his mouth, piercing my eardrums like the blast of a train whistle. He lunged at the tree trunk as if he wished he could climb. Thank goodness he couldn't. But he sure tried.

After a while, he quit barking. His ever-sniffing nose took him to the shopping cart where Tikky crouched within its steel confines. Barking like a maniac, the dog ran circles around it.

Tikky hissed and growled. Every time the dog got too close, Tikky swiped his claws through the steel mesh, even slashed the snarling nose a few times.

That only enraged the dog more. His bark became more frantic. Tikky could hold his own, unless the mangy critter got the lid off that cart, which was what he attempted next. He chomped on an edge of the board, scratched at it, barked at it, and tore at it.

I don't know who had attached that board, but it held even when the dog grabbed one of the wheels and dragged the cart around the clearing. Tikky yowled and held on. Every time that dog got his face too close, Tikky tore him up.

I stayed glued to the tree limb with Tabbert hanging over the tip of my nose.

And then Tabbert fell, and I couldn't catch him. Grabbing nothing, his feet swam in the air. He landed on the dog's nose, leaped, and hit the ground running. The dog took off after him.

Annoying babbler or not, I had to help my little buddy. I jumped down from the tree and dashed after the yelping hound that was now leaping furiously to climb another tree.

I sailed through the air and landed on the dog's back and dug in. It was then I realized Tikky had followed too. He clung to the hound's neck.

The dog turned from the tree Tabbert had climbed. He howled and rolled over and over on the ground. Clinging to a hulk of raging mutt isn't a fun battle. I about lost my breath every time he rolled over with me on his back.

He finally shook Tikky and me off, turned tail, and fled. I'd have chased him, but I wanted to make sure Tabbert was okay.

"Tabbert," I yelled into the tree. "You up there?"

"Who are you looking for? Your little lizard friend? Tasty little fellow." Tikky licked his chops and grinned.

Maybe I was agitated from all the excitement, or maybe I was just tired of his pomp and fluff. I turned and swiped the grin off Tikky's face and followed that up with a cuff to his right ear. (I'm left-handed.)

He fell backwards but immediately leaped to his feet. "Hey. I was just kidding."

I glared at him with my teeth bared. "Not funny."

For once, Tikky had the good sense not to grin again. There was a time when we'd have been at each other's throats, but a few months ago we'd worked together to save Gidget.

She was special. Because of her, somehow Tikky and I had sorted out our differences.

Still, every now and then he brought out the bad in me. I admitted to myself that wasn't a good thing and figured I should apologize for hitting him, even though I didn't want to. "Sorry I hit you."

Tikky shrugged. "Didn't feel a thing. You really ought to work out more." He sniffed and pointed. "Over there on that log."

I looked where he was pointing and spied Tabbert catching and swallowing a mosquito.

I ran to him. "You okay?"

"Couldn't be better." He made a motion to swish his tail, only it wasn't there.

"Missing something?" Tikky asked.

Tabbert looked over his shoulder and down his back. "Oops, mutt must have been closer than I thought. Oh well, it'll grow back. I think I'll head home. Take a rest. All that running and a nice lunch made me kind of sleepy."

"Come on," I said. "I'll take you. I've had enough excitement for one day."

Tabbert skittered up my leg and perched on my shoulder. "See you around, Tikky."

"Later. Hey, by the way, I recognize that mutt. That's Leroy. Used to live in that junkyard trailer at the edge of the woods, that is, before it burnt down. People up and left him. We met once. Came to a men-in-the-woods kind of respect. He goes his way. I go mine. You know what I mean?"

"Yeah, sure," I said. To be honest, I didn't really understand. I live in a clean, comfortable house with people who feed me, pet me, and let me watch TV.

"Anyway," Tikky went on, "I'm going to sneak over to Hudson's farm, see if I can't sneak in a meal with the barn cats. Maybe stay and play for a bit." He licked his paw and swiped it once over his forehead. "Later." He headed into the orange grove.

Tabbert called to him, "Hey, Tikky."

Tikky stopped and turned around. "Yeah?"

"Thanks."

Tabbert looked at me. He was so close, I could see my eyes reflected in his. "Both of you, for ... you know, keeping that bugger from getting me."

"No problem, reptile," Tikky said. "If anybody's going to eat you, I guarantee you, it's not going to be some mangy old hound."

He grinned, winked, and turned away. Tabbert's eyes squinted into tiny slits. I just shook my head.

As I slipped through the woods with Tabbert hitching a ride, we talked about the dog.

"He looks dirty and pretty skinny. It's hard to believe he has a domestic bone in his body. I mean, did you see those teeth? It doesn't look like he's brushed them in a while. And his breath is really bad like he's been eating rotten eggs or something. I could smell him breathing down my neck when he was chasing me."

"You're lucky he didn't eat you."

That thought sobered both of us, I guess, because we didn't talk again the rest of the way.

When the gutter downspout where Tabbert lived came into view, he climbed down my tail and ran across the yard as fast as his little legs could carry him. He'd had a fright today and was missing a piece of his tail. I was sure he'd be happy just to spend some time in the safety of his own home. No need to say good bye. I'd see him later.

I nosed through cat door, padded quickly past my cat tower, and then squeezed through the small opening in the sliding glass door to the air conditioned quiet of the house. Ahh, a nap on the back of the couch seemed like a promising idea.

I was just about to jump up there when a strange sight stopped me frozen.

What—was—that? Every hair on my back stood straight up. My throat constricted as I struggled to keep a growl from escaping my chest. I ducked under the couch and investigated from there.

On the living room floor in front of the end table, a lump of black fur lay on a fuzzy, checkered pillow. My nostrils sniffed double time. Antiseptic. A blue and white bandage wrapped around one back leg, and half the fur up the other back leg had been shaved off. Stitches crisscrossed its body in several places—across its belly, along one ear, under one eye, down the other leg.

A puppy—a mangled one at that.

What was it doing in our house?

Chapter 2

A puppy...

... sleeping in our living room, right there, plain as day. A black one, same color as me. Really? I needed time to think. Skittering backwards from my position under the couch, I snuck back through the kitchen and gobbled the few crunchies remaining in my dish.

Not that I had anything against dogs, but I wasn't about to let a complete stranger, especially a dog, have any of my food before we were officially introduced.

I cleaned my bowl and headed out to the patio to my cat tower, climbed to the top, and pouted a little. Sometimes you have to allow yourself to feel your stuff. What can I say?

"Hey, Clawed! Whatcha doing?"

Was there no peace in this world? I sighed. So much for pouting. Probably better to get this off my chest anyway.

I jumped down from my tower and hopped up on the ledge where only the screen separated me from Tabbert and the gutter downspout he called home. "You might not want to talk to me right now. I'm in a bad mood."

Tabbert dashed up the screen, caught a fly, and returned.

That annoyed me. "Are you interested in hearing or not?"

"Touchy," he said. "What's up?"

"There's a puppy in the house."

That got his attention. "Really?"

"Really."

"You mean, it's going to live with you?"

"I don't know."

Tabbert spun in a circle and turned yellow, something he did whenever he got excited or felt threatened. "Seems like we're in for some dog days. First the mutt in the woods, now one in your house. Thanks for the warning."

"This one doesn't look so good," I said.

"No dog ever looks good to me." He glanced over his shoulder. I suppose he was thinking about how he'd lost his tail that very afternoon.

"Can't be any worse than the one in the woods."

"This one's different."

"How so?"

"This one's clean, but one back leg is shaved and all stitched up. The other leg is wrapped in bandages from the hip to its toes."

Tabbert peered at me through the screen. "Dummy must have been chasing a car or something. I never have understood why dogs like to chase cars. You know how many dogs I've seen dead on the road? Plenty, let me tell you. Boy, do they stink when they start to rot. You know, the vultures love it, though. Road pizza. Ha! Get it. Why, just the other day...."

I raised a paw to stop his blather. "This one isn't dead. It's in our living room."

"How'd it get there? Boy or girl? What's its name?"

"I don't know!" Talking to Tabbert wasn't helping one bit. I was growing more irritated by the minute. I'd have gone inside, but the dog was in there. I could climb to the top of my cat tower, but Tabbert would follow; and I was pretty sure if I went for a walk in the woods that mangy mutt who had attacked Tabbert would be out there ... somewhere.

This was a catastrophe for sure.

As if he'd read my mind, Tabbert tried his best to placate me. "Maybe it's not staying. You know Sage and Ben. They rescue everything. Maybe they're just taking care of it for a while."

I snorted and nodded. Sage and Ben had rescued me from a house full of kids, dogs, cats, and other critters and brought me to this nice, quiet house. And then, they got a spider in an aquarium and turtles they'd saved off the road. They'd also given Gidget a home.

I didn't want to think about Gidget right now.

Tabbert babbled on. "I seem to remember you telling me that you used to love a dog named Marnie. Maybe you'll love this dog too."

"This dog isn't Marnie."

"Okay, whatever. I can see you're absolutely right. You're in a mood. You hungry or something?"

"No, I'm not hungry," I snapped.

"Sleepy?"

"No."

"Well, come on out. Let's go for a walk."

What if that fool hound was hiding out there? I was in between a rock and a hard spot. (I learned that saying on *Wheel of Fortune*.)

A voice that only I can hear often talked to me out of nowhere. "Think, Clawed."

The only way a dog could have gotten into the house was if Sage or Ben had brought it in.

I didn't want Tabbert to see my hesitation. There was nothing to do but face the situation.

"I'll go back inside and find out what's going on."

"Good idea," Tabbert said. "Let me know when you figure it out." He spun in another circle, like a dog chasing its tail. "Because I'm not coming in again until you tell me it's safe."

I couldn't blame Tabbert for feeling frightened. He'd already lost his tail to the mutt in the woods. He couldn't afford to get that close to another dog until his tail grew back, if it ever did.

He told me once that it can take six months to a year for his tail to grow back. Even so, it might not grow back again, ever. As it was, he had trouble balancing since he'd lost his tail. I could tell by the way he wobbled on the screen. At least he was still alive. That was all that mattered.

Maybe a walk would do me good. There were plenty of places to go in the woods besides the clearing. Hopefully, by the time I got back, that stranger in my house would be gone.

"I changed my mind. Let's go to Bling. See if we can find Gidget. Maybe she'll know what to do."

She was a smart one even if she did yowl a lot. That was just her way. We had lots of great adventures. But when she fell into a sinkhole that's now a pond at the edge of our yard—well let's just say, I haven't been the same since. I sighed.

I missed her. If I could just talk to her, maybe she would ease my mind. So many things were going on.

I felt relatively safe going to Bling. It was right in our backyard. That mutt in the woods wouldn't dare come this close to the house.

I hated to think what would happen if Sage caught sight of him. She'd start another rescue crusade.

My mind was getting carried away. Stinking thinking too much always brings trouble.

Tabbert met me at the rose arbor.

"Let's go." He dashed through the archway. I tiptoed.

The magical town in the garden touched me in a deep place. Sounds a little crazy, but I'd come to know Bling was there, just like lizards' tails come off and wiggle on the ground to distract their would-be predators. #Truedat.

What, a cat can't know about hashtags? Many times I've watched *Wheel of Fortune* and *Jeopardy*. I also sit on Sage's desk and read when she's writing.

I'm a smart cat. Not being arrogant. Just saying.

I followed Tabbert past the blueberry flax that borders the cobbled path meandering through Bling. Pink blossoms of the weeping hibiscus dangled over our heads. Monarch caterpillars munched on nearby milkweed.

Thorny bougainvillea tangling with the wisteria demarcated the outer boundaries of the garden and Bling.

Beyond that jungle of brush, the cobbled path became a pebble-lined streambed where an artesian spring gently erupted out of the aquifer and flowed over the pebbles through our side yard to a pond. Beyond that were the woods and the clearing.

Not going there, at least not anymore today. I almost stepped on Tabbert when he stopped and called out.

"Hey, Piggy Pomp. Have you seen Gidget?"

Piggy stopped polishing the bougainvillea leaves. "Not today. Hi, Clawed. How are you?"

"Fine." I still wasn't used to seeing the Blinglings with their crystal-clear faceted bodies and beady black eyes. For the longest time I hadn't even known they were there. It was still hard for me to swallow that Gidget was no longer a furry feline and had become one of them, but that's a different story.

"When you see her," Tabbert said, "would you tell her we're looking for her?"

"Sure thing," Piggy Pomp answered.

We continued along the path. I stopped and lay down when we reached the edge of the garden where it met the woods.

"Hello there."

Tikky. You'd have thought it was a party or something.

Ever-chatty Tabbert immediately let the cat out of the bag. "There's a dog in the house." He climbed my tail, scooted up my back, and stopped when he reached his favorite spot in the middle of my forehead just above my eyes.

Tikky sat back on his haunches. "Well, doggone it. It's not that creep from the woods, is it?"

"No." I repeated the story about the injured puppy sleeping in the living room.

"Wow," Tikky said. "What's up with that? Boy or girl? What's its name?"

"He doesn't know," Tabbert answered for me.

Tikky licked his paw and wiped his face, a rare action for him. Usually he didn't care if he was clean or not. "What are you going to do about it?"

"Leave him alone," Tabbert said.

"I'm talking to him, reptile. Not you."

All I'd wanted was a quiet afternoon by myself. I could see that wasn't happening. "I'm going home."

Chapter 3

Leroy remained hidden, …

… his gaze following the cats as they went their separate ways. His neck smarted where the big orange one had bitten him. He could smell his own blood, and that enraged him. He'd thought he and that cat had an understanding. Not anymore.

Every spot where the cats had clung to him with their razor-sharp claws stung like fire ant bites. His nose bled, too.

Now that they weren't working together as a pair, he could probably take one down. Problem was he didn't have the same energy he used to, and tussling with them had taken every last ounce of strength he had.

His stomach cramped. He farted. Whew! He buried his nose under his paw. Leroy couldn't remember the last time he couldn't stand his own stink.

He was hungry. The lizard would have been a tiny snack, but at least it was something; except, that little scamp was fast. From his hiding place in the brush, Leroy watched Tikky scamper through the orange grove toward Farmer Hudson's place.

Leroy had visited there a few times, tried to catch a chicken. Last time a couple pieces of shot had found his back side and now festered under his skin like abscessed boils. He'd tried biting them out but couldn't reach back that far, had rolled in the dirt with the hopes that he could scrape them out. Nothing helped. The sores would probably heal on their own, just like times before.

He wished he could say he was getting used to living in the woods, but he wasn't. He missed the junkyard where he'd lived since he was a puppy, even though his memories of those days were growing dim.

Where was the comfortable green couch, or the hole he'd dug under the broken-down Chevy? There'd been food every day … food. His stomach growled, and he farted again. Those two cats had put him in a foul mood.

He thought about the kittens that used to venture out from under the trailer where he had lived with Max. Barely had their eyes open. Squinting up in the daylight, they'd never seen him coming.

With a growl, he remembered the day their mother had come back and found him playing with her kittens.

She was crazy, that one. Jumped up on his back, stuck in all her claws, grabbed hold of his neck, and held on no matter how many times Leroy had rolled over on her or shook himself to get her off. Wasn't until Max came out and fired his gun that the wild she-cat finally let loose, grabbed her kitten, and ran to the woods.

Leroy had halfheartedly chased her to the edge of the yard but didn't go any farther.

The bite festered until Max's wife, Marcy, had washed it and put some foul-smelling yellow stuff on it. Man, that burnt; but it did the trick.

When the cops came and told Max to clean up his yard or get fined, he set fire to the trailer and the brush in the yard. Flames devoured the dry weeds, started on the trailer, and raced toward the woods.

Max let Leroy off the chain and told him, "Go on, git!" Max booted Leroy square in the butt. Leroy ran into the woods and dove under a log. He ran deeper into the woods when the fire threatened to burn the trees standing close to the edge of the yard.

When it grew dark, Leroy snuck back to what remained of his home. The charred remains were still hot. Not a drop of water came from the spigot that used to drip constantly, the plastic bucket always under it melted into a blackened lump. Leroy sat in the ashes and whined.

Where was Max?

Leroy hung around the yard for days. When it rained and Leroy couldn't find shelter, he ran into the woods where the thick canopy overhead offered him some respite.

He dug up moles, ate palmetto bugs and lizards, and took to sneaking over to Farmer Hudson's yard to break into the chicken coup. That's where he'd gotten shot in the butt with the pellets that were a growing irritation.

And now, the cats.

Leroy didn't like cats. Not one bit. If those two cats came around again, he might find out what cat tasted like.

Chapter 4

Lily…

… opened her eyes. Everything hurt. Her mouth was dry, but she didn't have the energy to get up and get a drink. She sniffed the air. Water was close by. She looked around the room. Nothing looked familiar. Her head fell back onto the pillow. So tired. All she wanted to do was sleep. Where was she?

She remembered chewing through her rope and chasing after her sister, Dottie.

Her human family was gone the entire day. She and Dottie had been tied outside. For a while, she sat in the shade and watched the squirrels run back and forth across the top of the neighbor's fence. A few times, she tried leaping after one, but the rope had yanked her back. She could fix that. It felt good on her puppy teeth to gnaw.

"What are you doing?" Dottie asked.

"Chewing through the rope. I made short work of Dad's work boot yesterday. This ought to be a piece of cookie. Don't you want to be free of it, too?"

"We'll get in trouble."

"No, we won't." Lily chewed until she was finally free. She ran circles around the yard, took a drink from the water dish, and sat back to watch the squirrels again. Only now they were gone to lunch or had decided to take a nap somewhere out of eyesight.

"I'm bored," Lily said. "You coming or not?"

"Oh, all right." Dottie made short work of her rope too.

After that, everything was pretty much a blur. They'd run out of the yard and sniffed their way through the neighborhood and out onto the highway.

When a squirrel dashed across the road, they both chased it. Being the bigger of the two, Dottie was faster. Lily ran close on her heels but not quite fast enough. Dottie was already across the road when a car had loomed out of nowhere, slammed into Lily, and catapulted her through the air.

Now, here she was, but where was here? She opened her eyes to slits. A pleasant fragrance overtook her, something warm like a field of flowers on a sunny afternoon. Movement on the other side of the room caught her attention. She tried to blink the blur from her eyes. Focus. She couldn't. Tired. Lightheaded. Something strange—this wasn't her family's house.

Lily tried lifting her head again, whined when the exertion caused severe pain, worse in her hips and back legs. She looked down at her body. Holy dog biscuits!

Her right leg was bandaged to the hip. Half her stomach and back end were shaved, and stainless-steel threads stuck out of her skin all over the shaved area.

A voice. "Are you finally waking up?"

Friendly enough, but not familiar.

"How are you feeling, sweet puppy? Hm? Do you want to try to get up?"

Lily's tail thumped once on the pillow.

"Come on, girl. Let's go out." A soft-spoken woman patted Lily's head, scratched behind her ears, and smoothed the fur down her back. "Come on, pretty thing. Get up. Want a cookie?"

Lily struggled to stand, wobbled on three legs, took a step, and, with the woman's support, remained standing.

"Good girl." The woman extended a tiny morsel.

Lily sniffed it. Her stomach growled, but the smell turned her stomach. She gagged.

The woman patted her head again. "That's okay, girl. The vet said you probably wouldn't be feeling too good for a few days. I'm sure you'll eat when you're hungry."

Lily whined. The woman knelt beside her. "I'm Sage. Ben and I are going to take care of you from now on."

From now on?

Sage called to her. "Come on, Lily. Let's go out."

Lily staggered forward, if only to follow the comfortable smell wafting off this lady. It made her want to snuggle up and sleep for a gazillion years.

By the time she'd done her business and returned, Lily was exhausted. She lapped a few gulps of water from the bowl beside her pillow, flopped down, and closed her eyes.

She might have fallen asleep except for what she heard next.

"Hey, Clawed. I see you hiding under there. Come here."

Lily opened her eyes. Sage was down on her knees and reaching under a chair. "Come on, Clawed. Come meet Lily."

When Sage dragged a hissing cat out from under the chair, Lily's eyes flew wide open.

A cat.

This wasn't home. There definitely wasn't a cat in Lily's house.

I wasn't ready to meet the stranger yet, but Sage obviously had other ideas.

"Come on, you big goof. You're going to have meet our new family member sometime."

The dog was staying? I tried not to claw Sage, but my emotions got the best of me. I struggled to get away from her grasp, scratched, growled. Unfortunately she was stronger, and I really didn't scratch her that hard anyway.

"Quit that. That's not nice, Clawed."

I growled again.

She picked me up and carried me over to the pillow where the intruder was sitting cattywampus-like.

"No scratching." Sage clamped me under her arm and held my front feet with one hand, squatted, and pet the puppy with her free hand. "This is Lily. Lily, meet Clawed."

The puppy quivered a bit and then yawned. Her eyes were dull, but I could see real interest in them. I didn't know what made her so sleepy, but I'd bet a week of crunchies that if she wasn't all bandaged up, she'd be chasing me through the house right now. I hissed and struggled to get loose.

Sage let me go. I turned and ran, but not too far. I didn't hide under the chair. Now that the pup and I had met, I wanted Miss Lily to understand something. She might be hurt and all, but this was my house.

I gave her my best strong meow, shrugged, and, without looking back, did my best to saunter out of the room as if having a dog around didn't bother me in the least.

If I could handle a mangy mutt twice her size in the woods, what could a banged-up puppy who could barely keep her eyes open do to me?

Chapter 5

Days and then weeks...

... went by as Lily slowly regained her strength. I could have won an award for my acting abilities. Although I kept a close eye on the puppy, I walked around the house as if nothing were different. She was moving around easier, staying awake for longer periods, and exploring her surroundings more and more.

After giving me his customary hello and petting, Ben gave the puppy a treat and sat by her every day when he got home from work. Traitor.

I was struggling with my attitude. As I've already said, I still missed Gidget, and I was none too happy that she'd been replaced, especially by a dog. Maybe I was even a little bit jealous at the attention Sage and Ber were lavishing on the dog. I admitted that to Tabbert later that afternoon.

"Dogs have always required more attention than cats," Tabbert said.

He and I were sitting in the shade of the bougainvillea bush, a great hiding place for Tabbert. The thorns were as long as he was, and anything trying to catch him in there had those to deal with along with the fact that he was faster than a speeding hummingbird most of the time.

"Is that supposed to make me feel better?"

"Okay, sorry. I get it. I'm just saying. You're a whole lot tougher than that sorry critter. I've checked her out."

"You have?" That surprised me because Tabbert had said he wasn't going in the house again until it was safe, and I still hadn't given him the "all clear."

"Well, if I waited for you to figure out if that dog is a friendly or not, I might never see her."

I should have known. You know how they say, "curiosity killed the cat"? Well, Tabbert was one of the most curious critters I'd ever met. I hoped curiosity wouldn't kill the lizard.

"So, what do you think?"

"I don't know yet. She doesn't seem very frisky. I mean, most puppies jump around, chase their tails, and chew things. But I guess she's still on the mend. She sleeps a lot. She's not limping as much, though. Is she going to wear those bandages forever?"

"Probably not. How many times have you been in since she got here?"

"A few. You think you're the only one keeping your eye on her? My tail hasn't grown back yet," Tabbert said. "I have to be careful."

The words were no sooner out of his mouth when our conversation was interrupted by a loud whine. We peered out from where we were sitting. Lily was staring out the patio screen at us.

"Uh, oh. That doesn't look good. What happens when she figures out how to jump out the cat door?" Tabbert scooted under the bush.

"Hopefully it's too small for her." I looked the other way.

"Hey, Clawed," Lily barked. That was the first time I'd heard her say anything. Interesting. I made a mental note. Sounded … did I dare say it—strong but not threatening. It seemed almost confident and at the same time—puppyish.

Sage came out the sliding glass door onto the patio. "Good girl, Lily. Want to go out?" Lily's tail thumped on the deck. Sage attached a leash to her collar, opened the door, and led her outside.

Tabbert was right. Lily wasn't limping as much. I scooted under the bush when Sage said, "Time to see how you manage yourself in the yard," and let go of Lily's leash.

As it was, it didn't take Sage much to catch her, but not before the Lily, yelping like a banshee, dashed straight at me.

I crawled under the thickest part of the bougainvillea bush. That sort of stopped her, but the barking fool pushed her nose into the thorny thicket as far as she could. Didn't seem to be anything wrong with her front legs.

When a thorn pricked the end of her nose, she yelped and backed off. Sage caught hold of her and clicked the leash back on her collar.

"No, Lily!" Sage must have seen me then. "Aww, you in there, Clawed?" She waggled her finger in Lily's face. "No chasing Clawed. Do you hear me?"

Lily sat and thumped her tail. Trying to look cute, I suppose. Must be it worked because Sage crouched down and patted Lily's head.

Horrors! Did Sage just let that mutt lick her face? That did it. I turned and ran into the woods.

Tikky found me sulking in the shopping cart in the clearing. "Whatcha doing, bub?"

I really didn't feel like talking. "Nothing."

"I saw that idiot puppy. You really going to let her ruin your life?"

"What's that supposed to mean?" Tikky had a lot of nerve saying that. He'd been a thorn in my side ever since I'd known him. We were friends only because he'd helped me try to save Gidget when she'd fallen into the sinkhole that was now the pond in our side yard.

He lived in the woods and smelled like—rotten something. Sage would have taken him in, but he didn't want that said he preferred being independent. Some independence. Sage kept a food dish for him out by the front door and every day he gobbled it up. I wasn't letting anyone or any puppy ruin my life.

"I mean, you've been pretty crabby lately," he said.

"I have a good reason to be."

"What? You like being crabby?"

I hissed and took a swipe at him.

He backed away before my claws could connect with his face. "That's what I mean, right there. That pup isn't here now, and you're still being crabby. Why don't you just be here, in these woods, enjoying the moment." He rolled on his back in the dirt from one side to the other. When he stood, he shook himself. A cloud of dust and leaves drifted across the clearing.

I sneezed. More miserable than before, I growled, "You're a mess. Leave me alone."

"And you're spoiled."

"You're spoiled," I said. "Have you smelled yourself lately?"

"There's nothing wrong with the way I smell. I kind of like it."

He then made the mistake of rubbing against me. I'd had it—with him, with Lily, with Sage and Ben, with everything. I leaped on him and dug my claws into his thick fur. Wasn't hard to do, seeing as how it was all matted.

Tikky didn't take it sitting down. One thing about him for sure—he may have been a skinny woods cat, but he was tough as nails. He rolled over onto his back and plowed me into the dirt.

All my frustrations came out. I bit his ear. He wriggled loose of my grip, turned around, and clawed my face.

"Is that the best you've got?" I snarled and landed a good one alongside his eye. We battled, hissed, kicked up dirt, and yowled.

I was just beginning to enjoy myself. It kind of reminded me of when I was little, living in some other house with my brothers and sisters. The thought must have eased me a bit, and good thing, too. Otherwise I may not have seen Leroy coming.

"Run!" I tore away from Tikky's grasp and scrambled up the nearest tree with Tikky hot on my heels. That mongrel woods stray yapped at us from below.

Tikky and I looked at each other.

"That was close," he said.

I didn't comment. This was a fine predicament. One dog at home, a crazy hound trying to climb the tree I was in, and a stinky, feral cat sitting on the branch next to me.

Things couldn't get much worse.

Wrong.

Leroy stopped barking and sat looking up at us. "If you think you're going anywhere, you'll have to get through me first." He smiled when he said that.

Tabbert was right. That dog's teeth looked bad.

"And, you say I stink," Tikky whispered. "I can smell that mutt's rotten breath all the way up here."

The sun was going down. My stomach growled. I wanted to go home. I peered down. Rot Mouth was still smiling up at us.

"Looks like it's just you and me, bub," Tikky said.

I buried my nose in my paws.

We didn't get down out of that tree until afternoon next day when Leroy finally wandered off. You'd have thought that episode would have kept me out of the woods.

Chapter 6

Obedience School…

… helped Lily's excitable behavior, but not a lot.

After the cast came off and the stainless-steel stitches were removed, Sage stopped giving Lily the sleepy pill. "She's a puppy. We've got to expect that she's going to be frisky. We can't keep her sedated forever."

"That's why you're taking her to obedience school, right?"

"Yes."

Once a week for two-and-a-half months, Lily climbed in the car with Sage and rode to the school where Wisney, the self-proclaimed Dog Whisperer, explained to the adults. "You're here to learn how to manage your dog, not to train your dog new behaviors. You're the alpha of the pack."

"I don't know about that," Sage whispered to Lily. "I just want you to stop chasing Clawed. Do you understand? The holidays are coming up and you can't be a terror in the house."

Lily stared at the treat in Sage's hand. When she finally sat at Sage's command, the treat was proffered which Lily quickly gobbled up. Sit. Cookie. Got that.

When Lily did what Sage asked, she received a treat. Lily had quickly figured out begging worked on Ben. He gave treats for free. Why didn't Sage?

"How old did the vet say she is?" Ben asked.

"Dr. Jen thinks Lily is about seven months old now."

"Makes sense, considering how fast she's healing. Good thing she's so young."

"She's lucky to be alive." Sage patted Lily's head. "Aren't you, girl?" Thump, thump. "No wonder you spoil her. Just look at those eyes. You're so pretty; yes, you are." Thump, thump. "Having Lily here will be good for Clawed. I wonder what he thinks about all this."

I heard my name just as I came in from the patio.

"Hey, Clawed."

"Meow."

That got Lily's attention. Me and my big mouth. I should have taken a page out of Gidget's book. Listen more. Talk less. Lily looked up at Sage, scrambled to her feet and limp-dashed across the living room after me side-sliding into a box of ornaments Sage had out on the floor. I wondered how she'd manage the decorated tree.

I jumped up onto the back of the couch. "Leave me alone." Where would I go if Lily jumped up on the back of the couch too? And what would happen if Sage and Ben went out and left me home alone with her?

Now seemed like an appropriate time to assert my authority as the alpha in the house. I tried the you-can-catch-more-flies-with-honey tactic. "Hey, pup."

Lily's tail shook her whole body as she stared up at me from the floor. "Hi, Clawed. Want to play? Huh? Want to?" She wobbled on three legs using her weaker back leg as a balancing point only.

"Maybe. But, you're bigger. I'm sure you'd never hurt me, but what if you accidentally bite me?"

"I won't, I won't." The tail-wagging finally knocked her over. Whining, she fell onto her side.

"Still hurts?"

"I'm okay." Lily was up on three legs again. "Want to play now?"

Lily sat back in that cattywampus way we came to recognize over time, leaning more on her left hip with the right leg splayed out to her side.

That leg that obviously bothered her most, the one the vet had casted, the one where the skin had been ripped back like stripping off a glove, and all the ligaments in the ankle had been torn.

Lily didn't seem to have any recognition of pain. She'd already chased me around the living room more than a few times. I'd gotten in a few swats. Although she yelped, jabbing my claws into the end of her nose didn't dissuade her from trying again.

"I don't really like to be chased," I said.

"Okay," Lily said. "What do you want to play?"

"How about hide and seek?"

"That sounds like fun. How do you play?"

"I count to ten while you go hide, and then I try to find you."

"That sounds like fun. When do we start?"

"Now." I closed my eyes and counted. "One...."

It took about thirty minutes before she found me sitting at the top of my cat tower. She leapt up, rested her front paws against it, and barked. "Hey. How come you're up there? I thought we were playing a game."

"That was a pretty good hiding spot," I told her. "I couldn't find you anywhere."

"Want to play again? This time, I'll count and you hide." Lily wagged her tail and barked some more.

"Lily!" Sage called from inside. "Get down."

Lily barked again. "But Clawed said he would play with me. Didn't you, Clawed? Tell her."

"Meow." Silly pup still hadn't figured out that humans didn't understand cat or dog language.

Sage brought out Lily's leash. "Do you want to go out, girl?"

She leaped and barked as if going outside was the most wonderful thing.

I had to hand it to Lily. Although younger, she was about three times bigger than me and had the exuberance of the Energizer Bunny even with that banged-up back end of hers. I believed that, in her excitement, she could do some damage with those pearly whites if she caught hold of me.

I shook my head. I missed Gidget.

 "Dude!"

Would I ever get a nap?

"You let that puppy in the garden?"

"Hello to you, too, Tabbert." I yawned. "I don't *let* that puppy anywhere. If I had my way, she wouldn't even be here."

Tabbert spun in a circle and turned yellow. "She's digging in the garden."

"So…"

"So? What if she digs up Bling? What about Gidget and all the other Blinglings?"

"They're magic, Tabbert. They'll be fine. They survived the flood, didn't they?"

I thought of the magic town just inside the rose arbor where the Blinglings live. Mostly clear, their bodies were faceted, like diamonds. They had beady black eyes and some slid when they moved, like snails. Sound incredible? I wouldn't believe it either if I hadn't seen them myself.

Gidget lived in Bling now. Only I hadn't seen her since she went to live there. It choked me up just thinking about it. I swallowed hard. "Remember when it rained for about a week and filled the sinkhole?"

"Yes, but…."

"You told me yourself, you saw them come out of that sinkhole and make their way back to Bling. You said you saw her. You weren't lying, were you?"

"No, but…."

"Don't worry then."

But seriously, Tabbert's comment about Lily digging in the garden worried me a little. Why was it that I could see Piggy Pomp and Joe and Steve but hadn't seen Gidget yet, not even in her new form as the Secretarycat of Bling?

What if Lily had damaged Bling and hurt Gidget?

"Why are you pretending you're not worried?" Tabbert asked.

Was I so transparent that he could figure me out that easily? "Okay, so maybe I'm worried. What can I do about it?"

"I don't know. You can climb out your cat door, can't you? Go outside and make sure she doesn't hurt anything."

I just didn't have the energy. I really felt like crying. Dr. Phil on psychology-talk TV says it's okay for boys to cry.

"Who made you boss? Why don't you do it?"

"She'll eat me."

For a second, I thought that might be a good thing. Wow. I really was grumpy.

"Sorry, Tabbert."

"For what?"

"Nothing. Never mind. If I go out there right now, she'll see me, and she'll chase me for sure."

"Then you can run around to another part of the yard. Her tether is only thirty feet."

"Go away, Tabbert. Leave me alone."

"This pity party you're having is really frustrating, Clawed. You're not the only one who misses Gidget you know."

"Yeah, but I seem to be the only one who hasn't seen her yet."

Tabbert sat back and frowned. "I can't help that."

"And I can't help it if the puppy is running around the yard."

Chapter 7

Skeeter...

... didn't really understand her purpose in life, but it had to be more than being a part of a complex food chain that meant she'd been born to be someone's breakfast.

She knew that mosquito hatchlings make up a significant part of the food source for migratory birds.

Right here in Florida, there were plenty of threats to her existence.

She'd survived the larval stage where she'd swum with other hatchlings in the birdbath and barely escaped a family of scrub jays that frequently bathed there.

Not to mention the fleet-footed lizards that used their tongues like whips. One second you were buzzing around just minding your own business, the next instant you were stuck to a lizard's tongue and gone, lickety-split, just like that. Skeeter had seen it plenty of times.

"We're not just here to be eaten by other animals," Skeeter's mother said. "We also pollinate plants when we drink flower nectar. That's a good thing, isn't it?"

Skeeter admitted that it was. While she loved the honeydew of flowering plants, Skeeter hated one thing with a passion. Blood.

"You're a strange one," her mother told her. "You have to like it. You need the protein from it to produce eggs. If you don't produce eggs, well— we could all be wiped out."

Skeeter doubted that refusing to drink blood from humans and animals would bring the mosquito population to the brink of extinction.

Maybe she didn't want to lay eggs. The boys didn't have to drink blood. Maybe she wanted to do something else. She didn't know what that was, but lately she found herself thinking a lot about it.

The way she saw it, every species had anomalies. Look at Bling. There were some totally unexplainable critters in there.

Some humans smelled good, some didn't. Skeeter liked hanging around the wonderfully fragrant lady who lived in the house. That didn't mean Skeeter wanted to bite her.

And lizards—some could turn different colors, others couldn't. A morsel in their food choices, Skeeter steered clear of them.

Since there were so many threats in the outside world, Skeeter decided to spend more time in the house. It seemed safer.

True, a cat named Clawed lived in there; but he wasn't much of a threat.

When a green lizard came in on occasion, Skeeter hid under the couch, but she hadn't seen him lately. Was it a coincidence that she hadn't seen him since the puppy had arrived? Wouldn't hurt her feelings one bit if either the cat or the dog ate him. One less predator to worry about.

Skeeter enjoyed observing the comings and goings in the house while sitting on Lily's warm ear. They had struck up a conversation one afternoon which had led to a friendship. Lily had agreed not to scratch at Skeeter if Skeeter would settle down and not buzz in her ear.

"Looks to me like you and the cat are still trying to figure out if you're going to get along or not," Skeeter said to Lily one day.

"What do you mean? I like Clawed," Lily answered.

"I've been studying your progress. Doesn't look so good to me."

Sage and Ben had left a bit ago with their arms full of packages. Skeeter finished a drink from the fresh-cut flowers kept in a vase on the dining room table. She was bored. Clawed sauntered by. Skeeter decided to rustle up some fun.

She buzzed down to the pillow where Lily had fallen asleep, buzzed around her ear and then landed on it. "Bzzzt. Hey! Lily. Bzzzt."

Lily looked up. "Huh?"

"I think that cat ate a snack that was in your dish," Skeeter said.

Lily struggled to her feet, dashed after the cat, and boofed him in the butt.

Clawed leaped up on the back of the couch. "I told you I don't like being chased."

"And, I don't think it's very nice of you to eat treats that were left for me."

"I didn't. And even if I did, which I didn't, if there was food in my dish, wouldn't you steal it?"

"Sage doesn't want us eating each other's food."

"I don't eat your food," Clawed said. "I don't like the smell of your dish. And anyway, what makes you think I had treats?"

"Skeeter told me."

"Who's Skeeter?"

"My friend."

"You talk to a mosquito?"

"So?"

"That's weird."

"You talk to a lizard. I've seen you."

The cat leaned over the edge of the couch and glared at Lily. "That's Tabbert, and you'd better not chase him."

"I can't tell the difference between him and the other green ones. They all look alike."

"There's a simple solution to that problem. Don't chase any green ones. As a matter of fact, don't chase any."

Skeeter flew off Lily's ear and buzzed around the cat's face. He shook his head.

Skeeter zipped out from under his chin and dive bombed him right between the eyes. Clawed swiped at her.

"Hey," Lily barked. "Stop. That's Skeeter." Lily leapt up, clutched the cushion with her baby sharp claws, and barked again.

"How would I know? They all look alike to me."

Lily's weak hind legs gave out. She dropped to the floor and whined, "Skeeter, come here."

Skeeter landed on Lily's nose. Lily looked at her cross-eyed. "Skeeter, meet Clawed. Clawed, this is Skeeter."

"Hi, Clawed."

Clawed didn't respond right away but glanced around the room. "Oh brother, now I'm talking to a mosquito. What next? If you bite me, you're done."

"I won't. I don't like blood."

"What kind of a mosquito are you?" Clawed snorted. "That's a good one. I'm tired. I'm going to take a nap." He jumped down from the back of the couch.

Unable to restrain herself, Lily nudged Clawed's bottom. Clawed turned around and swatted her face.

Lily yelped, "Hey."

"I told you not to do that."

Lily whined, "I'm sorry."

"Yeah, well, don't do it again."

"Gosh, what's got you so grumpy."

Clawed ignored her, jumped out the cat door, and climbed to the top of his cat tower.

Lily turned to Skeeter. "Did you fib to me?"

Skeeter buzzed around Lily's ears. "I was just looking for a little fun. I didn't mean anything by it."

"That's not cool." Lily flopped down on her pillow. "You shouldn't lie. Otherwise I won't ever know when to trust you."

"Yeah, yeah." Skeeter flew under the couch and settled on a spring. It was kind of like the brush in the woods, only there weren't any frogs or other predators. Even so, she'd have to keep an eye out for the reptile.

She didn't feel too bad about taunting Lily and Clawed. It had been fun, and she was pretty sure Lily would get over it.

Strange was rapidly becoming the new normal.

Chapter 8

It was almost Christmas...

... and I, Clawed, ordinarily agreeable and positive, hate to admit it, but I might have been a bit depressed. It didn't take a puppy to tell me I was grouchy. I felt it deep down in my bones.

My gut ached like I'd swallowed a stone, and my body felt like a hundred-pound weight. Mostly, I wanted to sleep, but maybe I'd go away for a few days. Not like forever. I liked Christmas too much, especially the treats, but lately I didn't feel much like eating.

Home was comfortable. Sage was the nicest, smell-good person I'd ever met. *Jeopardy* was my favorite TV show. I liked it when I lay down next to Ben and we watched it together. Usually that thought could cheer me up. But not now.

Lethargy smothered me like a too-tight collar, and a lump in my throat made it difficult for me to swallow.

Tikky had called me "spoiled." I didn't like that, but was it true? I needed to clear my head and thought about taking a little jaunt in the woods. Just grouchy enough, I wasn't about to let some mangy woods hound intimidate me.

"Where you going?" Tabbert ran beside me as I headed across the back yard.

"To the woods."

He didn't ask if he could come along. I tried not to let that bother me.

"What if that big dog is out there?"

"I'm not afraid of him."

When we reached the woods, Tabbert climbed up on my shoulder. I made my way through the clearing. Clean. Didn't look like any of the neighborhood kids had been camping lately, so I didn't bother searching for any leftover morsels of food.

I headed for the orange grove. The grass there was high and soft. Warm too, a wonderful place to take a nap or veg out while I gave myself a bath and let the afternoon slip by.

It wasn't going to be a quiet time, not with Tabbert along. Often way too chatty, nevertheless he was good company and probably exactly what I needed to get out of my head. Too dark in there sometimes.

"Anything new with the puppy?" Tabbert asked as I got settled.

"He's got a friend."

Tabbert spun in a circle and dashed over my back. I guess his body was too small to contain his excitement and that's why he did those acrobatics like he did. "Your humans didn't bring home another dog, did they?"

"No. It's a mosquito."

"Yum!"

I snorted. "I can't imagine eating a mosquito or why anyone would want to."

"For the same reason you eat that stinking mush that Sage puts in your dish. It's food. Mosquitoes are one of my favorites. Especially after they've been drinking nectar. Sweet." He licked his lips.

"Her name is Skeeter. Seems a bit of a troublemaker, though."

"All the more reason to eat her. What happened?"

"She said Lily ate some crunchies Sage had put in my bowl."

"And?"

"Lily denied it."

"Who do you believe?"

"I don't know. Lily seems innocent enough. Dumb like a puppy, but you never know."

We frittered away the afternoon with nonsensical chatter and napped. Tabbert lay nestled in my fur until my stomach rumbling woke us both. Suppertime.

"I'm going home."

We were in the middle of the clearing in the woods when Tabbert, hitching a ride, whispered in my ear, "Did you hear that?"

I stood as still as I could. A familiar whine not too far ahead made me turn tail and slink into a nearby thicket.

"That's him." Tabbert clung to the fur behind my right ear.

"Shush." Tabbert didn't need to be told twice.

Leroy entered the clearing.

I thought about going the long way home, out past Farmer Hudson's to the road; but any sudden movement might attract Leroy's attention. Tabbert would be absolutely no help at all if I got into a confrontation with yellow-fanged bad breath.

I knew better than to tussle with a dog four times my size, especially when I didn't have Tikky backing me up. Where was that fluffed-up fireball anyway? Most times when I went to the woods, he had an uncanny way of showing up, like he was part of the plan all along.

Not that day.

I raised my nose to the wind so I could figure which way it was blowing and hoped the dog wouldn't smell me.

Dogs have a nose for odors. They possess up to 300 million olfactory receptors, and the part of a dog's brain that is devoted to analyzing smells is greater than mine.

I lay motionless and did my best to slow my breathing. Quite the predicament I was in. Trying my best to move very little, I located the nearest tree. There was one close by; but if I were going to reach it, I'd have to get out of this thicket and make a twenty-yard dash. Last time I tangled with this mutt, Tikky and I were closer to a tree.

The kids had collected all the wood near the clearing for campfires, so there weren't a lot of places to hide. That scruffy fleabag was going to see me sooner or later if he didn't sniff me out first.

Sure enough. He lifted his nose out of the dirt, yelped, and headed our way.

"Run!" Tabbert said.

I turned quickly and got caught in a tangle of branches. I pushed through it, dug my claws into the ground, and bolted for the tree.

When I leaped for the trunk, Leroy sank his teeth into my back leg, yanked me backward, and clamped down hard. Something snapped. I cried out, couldn't help it.

I twisted around and dug at him with my other feet.

He shook me back and forth like a rag doll. Fire raced up my leg. I couldn't catch hold of anything.

When he body-slammed me onto the ground, every vertebra in my back cracked. Only sheer will gave me the strength I needed to claw at his eyes when he stuck his stinking muzzle into my belly. He pulled his head back. That gave me the moment I needed.

You know there's a God when you escape a situation by the fur of your belly.

I didn't know how much pain I was in until I reached the first branch way above his head. I gasped.

I took quick stock of my body. My mauled leg dangled from the branch. Obviously, my back wasn't broken. Otherwise I wouldn't have been able to climb and probably would have been dead by then.

At the foot of the tree, Leroy barked like a lunatic and leapt at the trunk until he could leap no more.

"I'm not leaving this time," he growled. "You got away from me once. It won't happen again even if I have to sit here forever."

Only a miracle would save me now.

Tabbert was no longer clinging to my fur. I hoped he hadn't gotten crushed in the brawl.

Although dusk slowly robbed the clearing of light, my vision was becoming clearer by the minute. We cats have the edge when it comes to night vision.

I peered over the branch to search the ground. "Tabbert."

Leroy stared up at me. "Don't try calling for help. You're too far from home."

I tried calling again, louder, "Tabbert!"

No response. The last thing I needed was to lose another friend, pretty much my best friend at that.

I was so tired. I wanted to close my eyes and sleep, but I was afraid I'd fall off the branch.

For sure, that would be the end of me. I peered over the branch again. Evil Eyes didn't blink. My leg was killing me, and every muscle ached.

I thought about Gidget, how she'd survived so many lives—nine to be exact. Seemed like I'd lived a dozen since the pup and Leroy had come into my life.

That was a sobering thought. Was I going to die? Would I go to Bling? Maybe then I'd see Gidget. I closed my eyes.

"Pssst!"

My fur rose an inch all the way down my back.

"Take it easy. It's just me." Tabbert appeared in front of my face.

"Jeepers, you're a sight for sore eyes," I said.

"You okay?"

"No. The bugger got me."

Tabbert scooted along the branch and then returned. "Uh oh, that doesn't look good."

"Bleeding?"

"Yup."

"I think it's broken, too."

"I heard him say he was going to sit there forever. How are you going to get down?"

"I don't know."

"I'll go for help."

Before I had a chance to say anything else, Tabbert turned yellow, completed a dizzying spin, and dashed down the back of the tree and off into the woods.

"Everything's going to be okay."

Why in the world would that internal voice of mine say that?

Chapter 9

To know your enemy...

...you must become your enemy. Sun Tzu wrote that in *The Art of War* a long time ago. I read it with Ben on his computer.

Why had that just come to mind?

Must have been the voice. Things weren't going so good at the moment. But, I'd come to rely on that still, quiet voice. Again, stronger this time. "To know your enemy, you must become your enemy."

I peered down at the ground. "Hey, mutt."

Leroy growled and leapt at the tree with a fervor that made me wonder if he could possibly climb it. I was pretty sure he couldn't, but he tried real hard.

When he gave up, he flumped back on his haunches and barked at me for what seemed like hours. When his voice grew hoarse, he finally stopped.

I figured he was getting thirsty. "There's a pond behind Hudson's farm."

He drooled and licked his chops. So did I. I was thirsty too.

"Ain't going nowhere."

What was the best way to get him to let his guard down? Dr. Phil always said to try to make friends. "I'm Clawed."

"Who cares?"

"What's your name?"

"Don't think we're going to be friends. I don't care who you are or where you're from. When you fall out of that tree, I'm going to tear you to pieces, and then I'm going to eat you."

I wasn't getting anywhere. "They're going to come for me, you know."

That got him. He looked over his shoulder.

I badgered him some more. "Yup, that's right. I belong to somebody. And, they're going to come looking for me."

At least, I hoped they were. I'd never been out all night before. Sage and Ben had gone to a party. They might not even notice I wasn't home.

I was pretty sure Tabbert wasn't going to be able to bring help. I mean, who was he going to talk to? He hadn't mentioned whether he'd ever spoken to Lily yet. And Sage and Ben? Probably not.

How was I going to break through to this dog? Leroy's bad breath wafted through the air to me.

He licked his back end and whined at the same time. He was hurting. Had to be.

"Do you have an injury?"

"I'm fine." He laughed. It was not a happy sound. "How about you?"

I could see that some of his teeth were broken and his gums were swollen. Like I said, my night vision is good. I was pretty sure the odor that hit my nostrils was coming from that set of bad teeth.

But there was something else. Every time he stood to glare at me, he growled and barked. When he sat down, he glanced at his back end and whined.

I licked my foot. The bleeding had slowed. The pain had grown.

I thought about Tikky and the time I'd hurt my foot chasing him out of the yard. I'd hated him then, before he and I became friends. I wished he were with me now.

I persevered, trying to reach common ground with the skinny dog on the ground below me. Oh, my aching leg. "I have to hand it to you. You got me good."

"Going to get you worse than that soon as I get hold of you."

"At least you can tell me your name before I die. You owe me that."

"I don't owe you nothing."

Patience is a virtue, possess it if you can, rarely found in dogs, even less in man. Or something like that. Didn't say anything about cats. I could outplay, outlast, and outwit this dog. I was sure of that.

Problem was, I was rapidly losing patience, opportunity, and the ability to stay awake.

On Dr. Phil's talk show, he had listed several ways to diffuse a bully. Number one—try humor.

There wasn't anything funny about being stuck in a tree with a mad dog raging below me. I couldn't think of anything humorous to say about my situation. It made me want to fight. And, I really don't like to. Last time I'd ended up getting hurt.

Number two—recruit a friend. Tabbert had gone for help. Where was Tikky?

Build relationships. That voice was working hard to get my attention.

I tried again. "What's your name?"

"None of your business."

"Oh, okay." I quickly gave up trying to be nice. "Then, you're a mean, grouchy bully."

He barked. "You don't know anything about me."

"So, tell me."

Silence.

It was getting dark. Usually by this time of night, I'd be watching something cool on TV. My stomach grumbled. My leg burned and throbbed. Maybe I was spoiled.

I was about to fall asleep when I heard him.

"Name's Leroy."

"Hey, Leroy."

"Just wanted you to know my name before you die."

Chapter 10

Tabbert slipped inside the house...

...through the crack beneath the cat door and skittered under the couch.

He hadn't ever talked to anyone in the house. Approaching a rambunctious puppy didn't seem wise.

A buzzing hum stopped him cold. Mosquito, his favorite snack. Where was it? He didn't move. Only his eyeballs rotated. Hummmm, bzzzz, mmmm, bzzzz. There it was, in the couch springs. He skittered up a wooden leg and flicked out his tongue. Missed.

The mosquito flew out from under the couch, swooped into the air, and buzzed around Sage's ear.

Sitting in her chair and sewing sock monkeys, Sage swatted at it. "Darned mosquitoes. That one's persistent. Almost every night, when I sit here, it buzzes around my head. Strange, it never bites me. It's still annoying, though."

Ben grunted and resumed channel surfing.

"What? No *Jeopardy*?"

"Nah," he said. "I don't feel like it. Have you seen Clawed?"

"No. I'm sure he'll be in soon."

"He'd better be. I still have mixed feelings about letting him go out."

"I know. I do too. Especially since we lost Gidget. I'm sure he's lonely. It seems like he pouts when he's cooped up inside. He's an outside cat. It's his nature."

"Maybe I'll feel better about it when we get a fence. I just don't want him getting hurt."

"Me neither, but…."

***

Tabbert zipped out from under the couch, dashed up Ben's pant leg, leaped onto his shirt, and onto the back of the couch where Clawed usually sat. He flared his dewlap and bobbed his head. "Clawed's hurt," he said.

"Sage, do you see this?" Ben asked.

That got Lily's attention. She sprang from her bed pillow, landed in Ben's lap, and snapped at the lizard.

"Lily, get down!"

Tabbert skedaddled. Lily followed, dove headlong over the arm of the couch to the floor, and scrambled across the tile in hot pursuit.

"Lily, no!"

Skeeter flew in circles above all the commotion. She swooped down and landed in Lily's ear. "Bzzzzz. That lizard just said Clawed's hurt."

Oblivious, the excited puppy scampered from one corner of the living room to the other. She sniffed every corner, pushed aside the floor-length drapes, and shoved her nose under every piece of furniture.

Skeeter buzzed louder in Lily's ear.

Lily whined, sat, and scratched.

"Lily, no lizards!" Ben hollered, but that made no difference to Lily.

Tabbert scooted out from under the wooden blind slat. Lily jumped up on the chair beside the window. The green lizard ran up the string that opened and closed the blinds. Lily barked, rammed her nose into the window, and pawed at the slats.

"Get down!" Sage's tone meant business. Lily jumped off the chair and sat, whining, staring at the window, her tail thumping the floor.

"I'll find it." Ben held a plastic kitchen container in one hand and an advertisement flyer from the newspaper in the other. "Sage, get Lily, will you? I'll catch the lizard and put it outside."

Sage grabbed hold of Lily's collar.

Ben slowly approached Tabbert clinging to the thin strings. When Ben lunged, Tabbert ran down the string and across the window sill.

Lily whined and tugged, but Sage held tight. Tabbert was quick, but Ben had him cornered. He clapped the container over the exhausted lizard and slipped the flyer under it, trapping Tabbert inside.

Ben picked him up. "Can you get the door?"

Sage dragged a still whining Lily to the front door and opened it. Ben stepped off the stoop and set the container on its side in the pineapple patch. Tabbert took off without a backward glance.

"Whew! That was close." Breathing heavily, he hid among the jagged leaves of a pineapple plant.

"He could have let the dog have you."

Tabbert spun in a circle. A mosquito circled just out of reach. "Who are you?"

"I'm Skeeter. And I suppose you're Tabbert."

"I am. I heard about you."

"You did?" Skeeter landed at the topmost leaf. "Does that mean you won't eat me?"

"I...."

The porch light came on. Sage stepped outside and shook a box of Clawed's food. "Clawed! Here, kitty, kitty, kitty."

Tabbert bobbed his head. "She can shake that box all night. He's not going to come home."

"Why not?" Skeeter said.

"Because he's hurt in the woods. A mean dog named Leroy bit his leg and has him treed. He can't come down. Otherwise, the dog will tear him to pieces. I heard him say it."

"And why would you care about a cat that would eat you given the first chance?"

Tabbert spun in a circle. "Clawed isn't just any cat. We're friends, have been for a while now. He never tried to eat me either. I trust him. Anyway, why do you care about that puppy inside?"

"She doesn't try to eat me. But, you'd probably eat me if I got close enough, wouldn't you? I mean, lizards eat mosquitoes like humans eat potato chips, don't they?"

"Well," Tabbert pressed his lips together in a think line, "... maybe not. Would you bite Clawed?"

Skeeter didn't answer.

"Well, would you?"

"Um, probably not." Skeeter flew to another branch a bit farther away. "I don't like the taste of blood. My family says that's not normal. So now you'll probably try to take advantage of that little bit of info and gobble me up like my life doesn't matter."

"So...." Tabbert dashed to the end of the pineapple leaf and snatched a small spider. He gulped it down and returned.

Skeeter had left his leaf tip and buzzed well out of the way of Tabbert's lightning fast tongue. "You're pretty quick."

"I know. Look at my tail though, or what's left of it. That dog in the woods almost got me. I barely escaped. That was a few weeks ago. And now that same dog bit Clawed and body slammed him into the ground. Clawed's leg is broken. I don't know how he managed to climb a tree, but that's where he's stuck right now. I was coming inside to figure out a way to tell somebody where he is. That's when the puppy saw me. Sheesh."

Tabbert bobbed his head and flared out his dewlap. "I can't go back in there. What am I going to do now?"

Skeeter flew in a circle over Tabbert's head. "You and I could make a deal."

"How's that?"

"I could talk to the pup. See if she can get their attention. On one condition, though."

"What is it?"

"You have to promise not to eat me."

"Okay, I promise."

"That's too easy."

"But that's what you asked me to do."

"How do I know you really mean it?"

"I wouldn't lie about a thing like that. If I really wanted to, I could have licked you up in a heartbeat. I have plenty of friends who trust me, just ask Clawed or Gidget."

"Who's Gidget?"

"She's my friend, too."

"I don't know her. How do I know she can be trusted?"

"You're a real doubting buzzer, aren't you? How do I know you can be trusted? How do I know you won't go back in and tell that dog where I am so he can find me and eat me?"

"I guess we're at an impasse," Skeeter said.

"I sure hope not. I'm just trying to help my friend, and right now it looks like you're the only one who can help. What do I need to do to prove to you I won't eat you?"

Tabbert cocked his head and looked up at the sky. "I know. You want to see my house? I live in the gutter spout. You don't have to come in. Then I'll show you Bling and where some of the best plant nectar is. Come on."

Tabbert scooted away and didn't look back. He had to believe Skeeter was curious and brave enough to follow.

Sage was still calling for Clawed and shaking the box of crunchies as Tabbert dashed around to the back of the house. There was no time to lose. He scooted up the gutter spout and waited.

"Bzzzt. Hummmm. Okay. Nice digs. Seems safe behind there, but I'm not coming in."

"Okay, whatever. Come on. I'll take you to meet Gidget." Tabbert ran down the gutter spout and dashed through the rose arbor.

Skeeter followed. The leaves of the rose bush climbing the arbor vibrated. She clamped her feet over her antennae. "What's that?"

"Have you ever been to Bling?"

"No, I can't say that I have had the displeasure. That vibrating is annoying."

"Hmph. Kind of like you buzzing around my head. Whenever a stranger comes through the arbor into Bling, the leaves give out a warning. Look, there's Joe and Steve. They're miceling brothers. Hey, guys!"

"Hey, Tabbert," Steve said. "We thought it was someone else. The alarm went off."

"Nope, just me," Tabbert answered. "Oh, and my ... uh, new friend, Skeeter."

"Is he cool?"

"He's a she. Skeeter is friends with the new puppy."

"You mean the one that dug a hole in the blueberry flax last week? That mutt has to learn some manners."

Skeeter buzzed around Joe's head. "That's my friend you're talking about, so you'd better be nice."

"You don't scare me," Joe said. "Your blood sucker won't work in here."

"Don't want it to either," Skeeter said.

"Really?"

"She means it," Tabbert answered.

"Well, if you trust her, Tabbert," Steve said.

"I do."

"Next time you should probably clear it with Gidget before you bring a stranger around," Steve said. "There are rules you know."

"Okay, okay. Do you know where she is? I'd really like to see her. I'm kind of in a hurry here."

"What else is new?" Joe said.

"No, really. Clawed's been bitten by a mean dog and his leg is broken. He's up a tree in the woods, and the dog won't let him down. I'm trying to get his people's attention so they'll go out and find him.

"I hate to be rude, but we need to be going." Tabbert scooted away. Skeeter flew a few inches over his head.

"Tell Clawed we said 'hi' when you see him," Steve called after them.

"Interesting," Skeeter said when they'd left the micelings behind.

"What is?"

"Those mice look like they're made of glass."

"They are, and they're not."

"That doesn't make sense."

"It's a long story, and we don't have time." Tabbert stopped in front of a four-foot-high shrub. Clusters of orange flowers brightened the tips of almost every branch.

"Wow," Skeeter buzzed from one, to the next, and to the next. "Smorgasbord."

"Told you." Tabbert waited a full thirty seconds. "Do you really need to eat right now? I've shown you my world. I hope you trust me now, because I'm still trying to find somebody who can help Clawed."

"Patience isn't your best virtue, I see." Skeeter burped. "Oops, excuse me."

"Will you go in and talk to Lily now?"

Skeeter eyed the honeysuckle blossoms again. "Do you think I'll be able to come back in here sometime?"

"Probably, as long as you're with me."

"You're not just trying to fatten me up so you can eat me when I'm not looking, are you?"

"You know what? Just forget it. I'll go talk to the Lily myself."

"And probably get eaten."

"Ben won't let that happen."

"And neither will I." At least four times larger than Tabbert, a transparent and faceted deer appeared out of nowhere. Antlers adorned his head like a crown of ice-covered branches.

"Stocker!"

"Hello, Tabbert. How are you?"

"F-f-f-fine, sir, Stocker, sir."

"It's not like you to be tongue-tied, Tabbert. Have you brought a guest?"

"Yes. Well, no. I'm trying to help Clawed, and I thought this dumb mosquito could help, but she doesn't seem very trusting."

"You know it isn't nice to call someone names, Tabbert, unless it is their name. Is her name Dumb?"

Tabbert hung his head for a moment. "No. This is Skeeter."

"Ah, yes. Skeeter."

Tabbert followed Stocker's gaze. Skeeter was frozen in mid-flight.

"Tabbert, did you know that lately Skeeter has been wondering what her purpose is?"

Tabbert shook his head.

"Just like you did before you realized how important your job is as a messenger."

Tabbert gulped. Although he was larger than most of Bling's residents, he still cowered in Stocker's presence. Magic wasn't something to mess with.

It had taken the destruction and restoration of Bling for Tabbert to realize that being a messenger between two worlds was critical. Stocker had been there then, and here he was now. Something important was going on.

"I'm thinking she's about to find out what her purpose is, don't you?" Stocker asked.

Not trusting his own voice, Tabbert nodded. His heart pounded in his chest. If Stocker said Skeeter was about to find out what she was meant to do, then it must be true.

Stocker stretched his nose toward the paralyzed mosquito. "Skeeter, I'm going to free you up now. Don't be afraid."

Released from the magic spell Stocker had cast over her, Skeeter flew in circles and loop-de-looped several times before landing on Stocker's shoulder.

"You're just like the mice," she said.

"Not exactly." Stocker transformed into a mosquito and, in the next instant, became a deer again. "They can't do that," he said.

"Eeek!" Skeeter darted away.

Tabbert's mouth gaped open. He hadn't even known Stocker could do that.

"I trust Tabbert," Stocker said. "You can too, Skeeter. I heard him tell Joe and Steve that you're his friend."

"When Tabbert introduced you as his friend, Skeeter, he gave you a gift of trust. Now, you're responsible for living up to that. Are you willing to take responsibility for the gift Tabbert has offered?"

Skeeter looked from the large stag to the green lizard. Was her purpose to help save a cat? Or was there more to it? She took a quick look at the honeysuckle bush again.

"There's more to life than a good nectar bush," Stocker said.

Skeeter gulped.

"It's a bit scary, isn't it? Trusting when everything inside tells you to turn and run. Time's a-wasting." Stocker pawed the ground and turned to Tabbert. "Do you have a plan B?"

"I was hoping Gidget might have an idea. Do you know where she is?"

"Yes."

"Where? Can you take us to her?"

"She's very busy right now, Tabbert."

"Oh." Tabbert's dewlap flared and he did several pushups. "When you see her, will you tell her Clawed is in trouble?"

Stocker nodded.

"I don't know else to do." Tabbert spun in a circle and turned yellow. "I guess I have to go in and talk to Lily myself."

"Okay, okay, I'll help," Skeeter said.

"You will? Great! Let's go then." Tabbert dashed toward the rose arbor.

"Tabbert?" Stocker called.

Tabbert skidded to a halt. "Yes, sir?"

"Leroy isn't a bad dog."

"Yes sir, Mr. Stocker." He scooted on his way.

This time, the leaves did not vibrate when Skeeter passed through the exit from Bling.

Stocker made his way up the hill to an overlook from where he often observed his domain, the town of Bling and the countryside surrounding it.

"Gidget," he called softly.

"I'm here."

"Clawed needs you."

"What can I do from here? I can't leave."

"Have you ever tried? Never assume anything, Gidget. Assumptions can be very limiting, and they're often wrong."

"What if they're not?"

"Did you survive nine lives only to still be afraid?"

Gidget stared into the dark. When she looked up, he was gone.

Chapter 11

Life's a fight…

… but not everyone's a fighter.

Mother had always told me, "Clawed, sometimes you have to fight."

Seemed like every time I got involved with someone, I ended up fighting their battles with them. It didn't always work out well, either. Like the time the sinkhole took Gidget.

Maybe karma was getting me. I hadn't been there for her. Now, she wasn't here for me. Neither was Tikky. Tabbert had gone to get help. I couldn't imagine what he could do.

So, there I sat on that branch over Leroy's head. I didn't like knowing his name. I'd been getting used to calling him mangy mutt, rotten breath, or anything else nasty that came to mind.

"Leroy" made him seem too personal. I didn't want to fool myself into thinking he was anything less than a very serious threat.

My leg was throbbing so badly I couldn't believe I felt like nodding off. What if I fell out of the tree? There was a strong chance that would be the end of me. I was pretty sure I wouldn't be able to run very quickly.

On top of that, blood loss was dulling my senses. I was feeling like I didn't really give a darn what happened.

But, of course, I did. I blinked in an effort to snap myself out of my pity party. Tikky would razz me for it if he knew. Tabbert would tell me it was a waste of time, and Gidget would tell me to get over myself. And here I was, missing her.

I yawned and peered down at the ground. Although Leroy was still staring up at me, he wasn't sitting at full alert any more.

"Hey, Leroy?"

He sat up again, whined, and glanced quickly at his injured tail region. "Why don't you come down from there. Let's get this over with."

I thought about not answering him. But then he barked and kept it up until I figured I'd better say something, if only to get him to shut up. His racket made my head pound.

"All that barking isn't going to help," I said. "You ought to go home." I immediately regretted saying that. The woods probably were his home.

"Let me down, and we'll let bygones be bygones. I won't come out to your world again." I meant it, too.

"As a matter of fact, if you don't quit barking, someone's going to hear and come to find out what all this caterwauling is about."

Leroy looked over his shoulder.

"Yup," I said. "I've got people, and they're probably looking for me right now." I hoped.

I could have bitten my tongue because afterwards, he quit barking.

"You have no idea what my life was like." Leroy stopped staring up into the tree and slumped to the ground. "I had people too. I had food anytime I wanted it. I had a green couch, an endless water bucket, and a great nap spot under a car."

Leroy had a home? "Why don't you go there then? Are you lost?"

"I'm not lost," Leroy said. "My people are gone. Fire burned the place down. Max kicked me and told me to git."

Served him right. Being left was no excuse to be mean.

"I'm a survivor. And when you either come down or fall out of that tree, you're going to find that out. So, stop dreaming of going home to whatever fancy-shmancy place you come from."

I yawned and stretched on the branch, a pain shot through my leg, a very clear reminder of what he'd done to me. I yowled, couldn't help it.

How long had I been up in this tree? The sun had gone down and the bit of light that came through the trees was fading fast. Tabbert was a resourceful little guy. Hopefully he'd find a way to bring help.

Tabbert darted under the flap on the cat door and scooted into the living room, momentarily mesmerized by the Christmas decorations gleaming everywhere. His image reflected back at him from every shiny bauble he passed.

Where was Skeeter?

Skeeter banged into the screen three times before figuring out that wasn't the way in. She sped around to the front of the house where Sage stood on the front stoop shaking a box of cat crunchies.

"Clawed! Here, kitty, kitty, kitty."

Skeeter buzzed around Sage's head. Sage swatted the air. Skeeter dodged right and landed on Sage's shoulder and stayed there until she went back inside.

"Find him?" Ben asked.

"No."

"He'll be fine."

"I hope so."

Tabbert scooted along the wall behind the curtain and waited for Skeeter's familiar buzz. "Over here," he said when he finally heard it.

Lily's head went up.

"Hurry up. Lily's awake. Where'd you go?"

"I couldn't get in," Skeeter answered.

"Why didn't you just follow me under the door?"

"You've got your way of doing things. I've got mine."

"Your radar was off, wasn't it?"

"Never mind."

"Ready to go with the plan?" Tabbert asked.

"I can't see how telling Lily is going to help. First of all, what makes you think she'll believe me? Second, even if she does, how's she going to get the people to understand? And, what makes you think they'll go looking for Clawed in the dark?"

"You just make sure you tell that pup to keep barking and tugging at the leash until they do. Get going. Next thing you know, she'll be chasing me all over the living room, and our window of opportunity will be gone."

"Okay, okay. But I'm not promising anything."

"You told Stocker you'd try."

"Yeah, yeah. Who is he anyway? He's just some critter in the garden. You looked afraid of him. Doesn't seem so scary to me."

"You sure looked scared when he froze you in mid-flight. He's the boss of Bling, the head honcho, kind of like the CEO, the president."

"All right, all right." Skeeter buzzed over to where Lily stared with bright eyes in Tabbert's direction. "Hey, Lily."

"Hey," she barked. "Is that Tabbert over there? Where've you been?"

Skeeter perched on Lily's nose. "You won't believe me."

"Really, was it fun? Huh? Can I go there? Want to go now? Where was it?" She sat up on the pillow and whined.

"Lily, you want to go out?" Sage patted Lily's back and swatted at the mosquito sitting on Lily's nose.

Skeeter barely escaped injury before landing behind Lily's ear. "Quiet down, and don't chase Tabbert. Pay attention. This is important."

Lily flopped down on her pillow.

"She probably does need to go out," Ben said. "I'll take her just before bed, and I'll call for Clawed one more time. You know Clawed. He can be ornery, especially when he gets outside. At least he's got Tikky out there somewhere."

"As long as they don't get in a squabble."

"I don't think that happens anymore. Do you?"

"Boys will be boys."

"Bzzzt. As I was saying," Skeeter said. "I think I know where Clawed is."

Lily's ears perked up. "You do?"

"Gosh, will you ever settle down? Tabbert told me Clawed's in the woods. Leroy bit him and broke his leg. Has him treed and won't let him down."

"Who's Leroy?"

"A big, mean dog in the woods."

Lily whimpered but cut it short when Skeeter did a loop-de-loop in front of her.

"Shhh."

"Sorry," Lily whispered. "What are we going to do?"

"You …" Skeeter did one more loop and landed between Lily's eyes, "are going to whine to go out. When they take you, they're going to call for Clawed like they've been doing. Right then, you've got to bark with everything you've got and tug at the leash like you know where he is. Tabbert and I will follow you out. He'll lead the way."

Lily whined. "It's dark out."

"Tabbert can see very well at night, and my sense of smell is superior."

"But,…" Lily whined again.

"What are you, a baby?"

"No."

Skeeter flew around Lily's head. "Haven't you been trying to make friends with Clawed?"

"Yes, but.…"

"Well, now's your chance."

"You believe a lizard? What if Tabbert's just trying to get rid of me? He probably hates me because I chase him."

"Yeah, about that."

"What?"

"You've got to quit doing that."

"Why?"

"Because it's not fun."

"It is to me."

"You're not the only one in the world. Sometimes you have to take others' feelings into consideration."

"I'm surprised the lizard didn't eat you."

"He promised not to if I came in here and asked you to help. You ready?"

"Ready."

Skeeter located Tabbert on top of the front door trim and flew a figure eight in the air.

Tabbert bobbed his head up and down and did pushups.

Lily whined, softly at first, and then louder. She ran to the door and pawed at the glass.

"Okay, girl, I hear you." Ben got up from the chair. "Do you think she'll run if I don't put the leash on her?"

At the same time Sage said, "Yes," Ben opened the door. Lily charged out into the yard.

"Lily!" Ben called. "Stop!"

Free of the restraining tether that usually choked her, Lily dashed up the street.

"Lily!" Ben ran back in the house, grabbed a flash light and Lily's pink leash, and took off after her.

Sage called from the open front door. "Wait! Bring your phone. I'll text you if she comes home."

Tabbert and Skeeter hid in the bougainvillea bush.

"What a knucklehead, and right now I don't care if it's not nice to call names."

"Who are you calling a knucklehead?"

"Both of them. That dumb puppy for running off and Ben for trying to chase after a dog that's black as night."

"Yup. What are we going to do now?" Skeeter asked.

"Wait and see who comes home first. Got any better ideas?"

"What about that glassy-looking buck in the garden?"

"Stocker?"

"Yeah, him."

"He doesn't usually get involved in the day to day stuff. But, maybe Gidget will. Come on."

Tabbert spun in a dizzying circle and ran off into the night.

Skeeter took off after him, Mach 1. "Wait up!"

Chapter 12

There's nothing like...

... running free with no restraint.

Lily seemed to have forgotten her fear of the dark. She ran almost as well as any dog could even though just a few short months earlier she'd been hit by a car.

So many smells. She stopped briefly to sniff a possum scent, dashed off, stopped again to pee on raccoon droppings, and sprinted away once more. It wasn't until the scent of a cat brought her to a halt that she remembered.

"Oh, my gosh! I'm supposed to be looking for Clawed." She looked around. Amazing how well she could see at night. Why had she been so afraid to come out? But where was home? And she had no idea where Clawed was.

Lily ran up one street and down another. After running through yards and in and behind several houses, she came to a tree line. She stopped and raised her nose to the air. Different smells in there. Should she go in the woods or try to find her way back to the house?

Surely, Skeeter and Tabbert were still waiting. Only Tabbert knew where Clawed was. How long had she been gone from the house? Were Sage and Ben looking for her and Clawed by now?

Hoping to hear a familiar sound she could hone in on, she strained to listen, twitching her ears.

Crazy-like dog barking came from deeper in the woods beyond the tree line. Hadn't Skeeter said Clawed had been hurt by a big dog and had climbed a tree to get away from it?

"Clawed," she barked.

She barged into the forest, stopping only once to listen and get her bearings. No more barking.

Trees loomed like menacing monsters around her. An owl hooted overhead. She flinched and tucked her tail between her legs. Lost, she was desperately lost.

Her only hope was to keep moving. Every twig that snapped under her feet frightened her. Every noise made her cower.

Then she saw him, in a clearing, a lean, hunk of mean dog staring up into a tree. Leroy didn't look as big as she'd thought he would. But he did look angry.

Lily dropped to her belly, disappearing into the dense underbrush, and followed his gaze. Clawed clung to a branch high up, one back leg hanging limp, the other tucked beneath him.

Lily bit her tongue to keep from barking. She looked over her shoulder. This had to be close to home. But which way?

Clawed would know. He'd been out here plenty of times. Lily recognized the same smells he usually came in with after one of his jaunts. Sure would be nice to be able to come and go like that.

What was she thinking? Right now, she wished she was home.

Nope. She had to figure out a way to distract that dog.

But he looked mean, and his growl was heart-stopping. Lily whined. The mongrel snapped his head around and glanced in her direction. Oops. She really had to stop talking out loud so much.

She crouched low in the bushes and did her best not to move, slowed her breathing, forced herself not to blink.

After what seemed like forever, Leroy turned his attention back up into the tree.

Think. What could she do to distract him and still be safe? Something smelled bad. She peered through the shrubs. Leroy rolled onto his side, stretched to lick his butt, and whined.

A nasty odor wafted Lily's way. Maybe there was something to a bath after all. That guy stunk.

She snapped to attention.

Clawed was leaning over the side of the branch and looking down. "Hey, Leroy. How'd you get hurt?"

"None of your business."

"Go find your people. They can take you to the vet. Get you feeling better."

"I already told you. I don't have people anymore. I don't need to feel better." Leroy growled. "I just need you to get down out of that tree. You will, sooner or later." He jumped up again, set his paws against the trunk like he wanted to climb the tree, but fell back to the ground with a whine when his bottom hit the dirt with a jolting thud.

Lily pushed her nose through the bushes. Leroy must be hurt. Maybe he couldn't catch her. Clawed needed to get out of that tree. He wouldn't be able to do that unless she distracted the dog's attention.

Muscles trembling, she tensed and prepared to dash across the clearing, past Leroy, and keep on running. Hopefully, she wouldn't get lost in the woods again once she got past the tree Clawed was in.

The owl hooted again.

Lily took a deep breath and sprang into action.

Like a flying demon, a black shadow approached Leroy's rear flank, barked once as it passed him, and disappeared into the bushes.

"Told you," Clawed said.

Leroy ran around to the other side of the tree. "Who's there?" He stood alert, sniffing, straining to see in the increasing darkness.

"A ghost," Clawed said over Leroy's head. "Come to haunt you."

"I'm not afraid, and I'm not leaving." Leroy stayed stared up into the tree.

Lily ran a long way, branches, palmetto fronds and berry bush thorns tearing at her fur before she finally stopped. Nothing chased her. All was quiet, as if every living thing held its breath waiting to see what happened next. Only the wind whispered in the tree tops. Her heart pounded.

She hunkered down into the underbrush to catch her breath.

Overhead, through a thick canopy of branches, bright stars twinkled. The silhouette of a big horned owl stood out against the clear, night sky.

"Hoot … do it again."

"What?"

"Hoot. Go on back. He's still there. Nip him in the tail this time. That'll distract him."

Really? Lily didn't want to get that close to the stinking mutt again. Leroy was bigger, probably stronger, too. She didn't want to run past him another time. The element of surprise was no longer in her favor. Maybe if she waited awhile.

Going back to the clearing would take her in the same direction she'd come. Was that where home was? Sage and Ben would worry if she didn't come home—especially with Clawed gone, too. Why, oh why, had she barged out the front door in the middle of the night?

But she had to help Clawed, and Leroy seemed determined to stand his ground.

She took a deep breath and slowly let it out. "Okay, Mr. Owl. Here goes."

Making as little sound as possible, she followed her own scent, sneaked through the brush, back the way she'd come. Once she reached the edge of the trees, she swallowed the fear gathering in her throat. She growled, bolted into the clearing, and headed straight for Leroy.

Her claws tore into the loamy forest floor. She barked and charged like a roaring lion. As she passed Leroy at full speed, she nipped him on the rump.

"Yow!" Leroy sped after her.

Lily looked over her shoulder. How was he keeping up?

Somewhat slowed by her own still-healing injuries, Lily managed to stay one length in front of his gnashing teeth. She had no idea where she was going.

Chapter 13

Apparently, Tabbert ...

... had come through for me.

I looked around the clearing and listened to the sounds of the retreating dogs. Hmph—Lily. I hadn't thought she had it in her.

My night vision being better than any dog's, I'd seen her arrival and first attempt to distract Leroy, which hadn't worked.

I hoped she and Tabbert had a plan B.

Watching her streak through the clearing not once, but twice, brought a flood of emotion to my overwhelmed and dulling senses. I swallowed hard.

"Get out of the tree," my inner voice insisted.

I had to be gone by the time Leroy got back, if he came back. I couldn't take any chances.

Two problems, though. My leg hurt like crazy. I wasn't sure it would support me while I climbed out of the tree. The other problem—Lily had led Leroy in the direction of home.

I had to take a different path. I didn't want to think about what Leroy would do to me if on his way back he smelled me in the bushes.

I tried hard to dismiss the thought. I wasn't staying in the tree another minute. Everything else would happen as it may.

By gobwinkies, it sure hurt climbing down. When I reached the ground, I had to rest to catch my breath. Once I did, dragging my hurting leg behind me and stopping often, I headed for home.

Every time I squeezed under a log or hopped over one, the pain tore at me. I grew more tired by the minute. Gasping, I stopped again.

"Keep going."

Startled by the voice, I flinched. The sudden movement shot a lightning bolt through my broken leg. "Yeow!" And in my next breath, "Gidget?"

I stretched my eyes open as wide as I could, straining to see my friend in the dark. My nostrils flared. "Where are you? How did you get here?"

"Keep moving and quit babbling like Tabbert."

"Hey, I don't babble," Tabbert caught my tail and climbed up on my forehead.

Gidget didn't say anything more. She'd always been a cat of few words. I limped on. Gidget would show herself when she had a mind to.

She was there. That was all that mattered.

"Skeeter," Tabbert said. "Go find Lily."

I hadn't seen her hovering about. Skeeter flew away and left me with my two best friends.

Chapter 14

Somehow...

... I managed to make it home. Right about the same time, Lily got there, too, with Skeeter's help, I was told later. Gidget left me at the front stoop seeing as how I didn't have the energy to jump through the cat door.

"When will I see you again?" I called to her as she slid away. I'd never get used to seeing her like that—like a Blingling.

She didn't answer me, and, for the moment, I didn't care. All I wanted was to get into the house.

When Lily barked and scratched at the door, Ben let us in. "Lily! Where have you been, silly dog? Whew, you stink." Then he saw me. "Clawed! Sage, Clawed's home. He's hurt."

It was my turn to be all bandaged up.

Our vet, Dr. Furby, was the emergency vet on call. He didn't seem very happy to see me again. "What kind of trouble have you gotten yourself into this time?" He patted my head. "Last time you were here, you were injured, and here you are again."

"Meow." I wanted to tell him not to patronize me, but Leroy's bite and my broken leg hurt like the bejeebers.

"Looks like a canine bite," he said. Getting a shot in my hip was like a mosquito bite compared to the pain when the doc washed the wound and put the cast on. "It's a clean break. Clawed has a broken femur. It should heal in about a month."

Dr. Furby waggled a finger in my face. "I know how your people feel about you being outside, but you're not going out for a while, at least three months. Doctor's orders."

I didn't feel like going out anyway.

After spending hours in the woods and half the night at the vet's office, I was glad to be home and let Sage pamper me.

Without the strength to jump up on the back of the couch, I was relegated to Lily's floor pillow.

"You need to give Lily a bath," Sage said.

"Now? It's late." Ben's whine almost sounded like Lily's.

As groggy as I was from the vet shot, I could smell her, too. Yuk! She must have found a pile of dung, or maybe some of Leroy's rot had rubbed off on her.

"Yes, now," Sage insisted. "She's not going to rub that stink off onto my clean rugs."

Ben grabbed Lily's collar and dragged her into the shower.

Ten minutes later, soaking wet and smelling much better, Lily ran out of the bathroom with her tail between her legs and plopped down on the rug next to me. I'd have bet a whole bag of cat crunchies that she'd much rather burrow into the couch cushion. Within seconds, she was snoring. I hadn't even thanked her for rescuing me.

Within days, I was up and limping around the house. The day after Christmas, when Sage and Ben had gone to see *Star Wars: The Last Jedi* (wished I could have gone), I woke Lily from a nap.

She looked at me from the couch and yawned. "You okay?" she asked.

"Yes." I swallowed a Christmas treat I'd gotten in my stocking. "I wanted to tell you something."

"Got anymore treats?" She yawned again. Afternoon was her nap time.

"Are you listening?"

"Yes." She rested her head between her front paws.

"Thanks."

"For what?" Lily jumped off the couch, came to me, and licked my face. For once, she didn't try to boof me in the behind.

"For helping me out in the woods." I wanted to tell her not to lick me like that, but somehow it didn't seem like the appropriate time.

My broken leg was itchy under the cast. The bite wound was healing.

"No problem. I wouldn't have known you were out there if Skeeter hadn't told me. She and Tabbert cooked up the plan."

"That was pretty brave of you to run in front of Leroy like you did."

Lily scratched behind her ear. "Aww, jeepers. It was pretty scary. I wonder where Leroy came from. I thought you guys said he was just a woods mutt."

Leroy had told me some of his story, but who knew what to believe. He looked and smelled too grungy to belong to anyone who cared about him. I didn't know how long he'd been on his own.

Before I had a chance to think about it anymore, Lily ran to the front door and set up such a caterwauling I about jumped out of my skin.

Through the full-paned glass, we observed a man approaching the front stoop. Lily barked like a maniac.

I clamped my paws over my ears and hissed. "Hush up!" She didn't.

The man rang the bell, waited, knocked, and rang the bell again. He finally laid something down on the stoop and left.

Lily didn't quiet down until his car was out of sight. Annoying as it was, I was kind of glad she barked like that. I heard on the news that a dog in the house is a deterrent for thieves.

She'd just hopped up on the couch again when Tabbert dropped in. "Hey, y'all."

Lily's tail thumped on the cushion, and her eyes grew as bright as shining crystals. She no doubt wanted to chase him and could barely contain herself.

Skeeter buzzed around my ears. "Lily better not chase my friend."

"Sorry, but I can barely understand what you're saying with all that racket you're making." I swatted at the annoying mosquito, purposely missing. Whiskers! Her buzz was irritating.

Apparently, Tabbert and Skeeter had come to terms. Maybe I should too. "I know why you buzz like that." I had learned it on *Jeopardy* just last night.

"Because I do, that's all." Skeeter buzzed up to Lily and settled on the pup's ear.

"Did you know that female mosquitoes can beat their wings up to 500 times per second."

"Who's counting?"

"I'm just saying. Anyway, I never asked you how you found Lily the night you all came to rescue me."

"Easy, I smelled her." Skeeter loop-de-looped around my head.

"What about Leroy?"

"He chased us but couldn't keep up. He must really be sick."

I turned to Tabbert who had scooted up onto the pillow. "Hey."

"How're you feeling?" he asked.

"Better."

He climbed up on my head and settled between my ears. "What are we going to do about Leroy?"

"I don't feel like talking about that right now, if you don't mind." I glanced at my bandaged leg. "I don't imagine I'll be going out anytime soon anyway."

"Sure, you will. You're young, resilient. Naturally made." He spun in a circle, bobbed his head, and did pushups on my forehead. I about went cross-eyed trying to look at him.

The front door opened.

Tabbert scooted under the couch. Lily quickly hopped off it.

"Clawed, Lily. We're home." Sage always called to us when she came in. I missed the days when she'd called to me and Gidget.

"I picked this up outside." Ben showed Sage an envelope. He ripped it open. "It's the fence estimate. It sure will be nice to let Lily out without having to put her on the leash all the time. The letter says they can start tomorrow. I'll give them a call."

A fence?

Lily gave me a big smile.

I shook my head and swallowed a growl. A fence caused all kinds of problems for me. I liked my freedom. It was a don't-fence-me-in kind of thing.

Would I have to jump the fence every time I wanted to take a walk, not that I was going to anytime soon. That wretched Leroy came to mind. I had mixed feelings about him; anger about how he'd hurt me, sympathy that he'd been left behind by his people. That still didn't give him an excuse to be vicious.

By the end of January, the fence was installed. Five feet high, black chain-link, it surrounded the entire backyard. I was feeling so much better, I'd taken to climbing up on my cat tower. I was getting the hang of dragging my bandaged leg around. I looked around the yard. Nice and quiet, except for the cicadas. I yawned.

Lily was in seventh heaven. I could tell by the way she tore around the yard like she'd never been hit by a car. I felt sorry for the Blinglings whenever she romped through their garden and chased lizards. No doubt Gidget....

At the thought of Gidget, my brain shifted gears. I hadn't seen her since the night she walked me home after my run-in with Leroy.

I wished I could talk to her again, but that would have to wait even though I finally had my cast off. My leg was still bandaged, and I couldn't imagine hopping out the cat door and going to Bling, let alone climbing a fence even though Sage and Ben were already talking about letting me go back outside. They were getting tired of me scratching at the door jambs. I couldn't help it. I needed outdoor time.

Lily dashed by, yelping and whining.

A squirrel chattered as it ran along the top of the fence. That little rodent sure was quick. Back and forth, it teased and taunted Lily.

She lunged at the fence. Next thing I knew, that silly mutt was climbing it.

She jammed one front paw into a diamond-shaped link, pulled herself up, and jammed the other front paw into another link. One after another, she kept doing that until she reached the top and hauled herself over.

Dropping to the other side, she ran off into the woods announcing to the entire world that she was out to get that squirrel.

I couldn't think of one single thing that had that much control over my good common sense.

Tabbert ran back and forth across the screen in front of my face. "Did you see that?"

"Yup. So much for obedience school."

Tabbert scooped up a fly and swallowed it. "What's she going to do when she comes home? Do you think she'll climb back in?"

"She'll be okay. It's not like she hasn't been in the woods before. She'll probably whine at the front door."

No way I'd ever whine at the front door like a dog begging to be let in or out. Oops. Internal voice reminded me that just recently I'd been at the front door hoping to be let in. I tried to whine. My meow came out like I had laryngitis.

"You have a sore throat or something?" Tabbert asked.

"No."

"So, what about Lily?"

"I'm not going to worry about her."

Turned out I should have.

Chapter 15

Such smells...

... everywhere, all kinds: lizards, bird doo-doo, turtle trails. Where had that pesky squirrel gone? Lily didn't know which way to turn first. She stopped to catch her breath.

Nose in the air, she glanced around and found herself in an orange grove that seemed vaguely familiar. She laid down in the deer grass under a tree, closed her eyes, and panted until she cooled off.

Cicadas buzzing in the warm shade lulled her to sleep. She dreamed of running through fragrant fields and being stuffed in a car on a long sleepy drive.

She dreamed about eating colored eggs she found hidden in the yard, being tied to a tree, chewing through the rope, and chasing her sister through yards, across the road....

A low growl followed by a pained yelp pulled her out of the dream. Listening, she twitched her ears left and right. The sound came from the edge of the woods. She lowered her head into the grass. There was only one thing worse than the smell of antiseptic on her leg, and she recognized it immediately. Leroy.

Staying low to the ground, she gathered her legs under her. Prepared to turn tail and run if necessary, she waited. The growl turned into more whining. Trying hard to see where Leroy was, she peered through the grass, crept forward a few feet, squinting hard until she finally spied him.

He was trying to lick his back-end near his tail where an open wound festered. Digging into the soft, loamy ground with his front paws, he twisted his body into a taut curve, like a roly-poly, and stretched to reach the oozing injury.

He was so tightly balled up that he lost his balance and fell over onto his back. He growled, whined, and then tried to reach it again.

Sage and Ben could help. Lily dashed through the grass and stopped within a few feet of where Leroy struggled, twisted like a pretzel trying to reach the injured spot.

"Dude. You okay?"

Mistake. The second she spoke, Leroy unwound himself and bolted toward her. Lily spun around and ran back into the grove—and beyond.

She turned once and found Leroy practically on her heels. How was he keeping up? She put forth more effort. "Ow," she yelped. Her back leg muscles screamed from the pain of exertion she hadn't used since she'd been slammed by a car.

She sped out of the grove and crossed the muddy shore of a cattail-studded cow-pond. At a dead run, she ran into a field where the loud rumbling of a haying machine drowned out the pounding in her heart. Shoulder-high grass whipped her face as she raced through the field.

Lily dashed into the open just as a monster tractor with a rotating cylinder of threshing blades bore down on her. She retreated in the nick of time and almost fell into the gnashing jaws of Leroy's rancid mouth.

Changing direction, she sped away from the thrumming drone of the tractor until, once again, she found herself in the clear running toward a huge, red barn. The door gaped wide open. Without slowing, she ran toward it, not once looking back to see if Leroy was still following.

She barreled into the barn and might have plowed into the opposite wall if not for a crowd of hissing cats. She slid to a stop.

"Whoa there, puppy dog." A white-haired, slump-backed horse towered over her. "Where do you think you're going?"

Hissing cats with fangs barred and ears flattened against their heads surrounded her on all sides. Lily glanced back over her shoulder toward the barn door. At least the huge animal wasn't snapping its teeth. She cowered.

The horse lowered its head and huffed in Lily's face. "Somebody chasing you?"

Afraid to move, Lily barely nodded. She'd never seen a live horse before. Wide-eyed, she glanced at the cats who, for the moment, weren't coming any closer; but that didn't mean they wouldn't. There seemed to be no escape unless she took her chances running past their barbed wire claws or under the horse's tree-stump legs

She decided to take her chances inside rather than go back out. No telling where Leroy was.

In a posture of submission, she crawled on her belly toward the pile of hay behind the horse.

"Decided to stay a while, huh? Go on, then." The horse stepped aside to allow Lily a clear path. "My name's Nel." She turned to the curious cats. "Let's not be rude to our guest. You know what it's like to be chased. Back off. Give the pup some breathing room."

Chapter 16

Leroy stopped...

...at the edge of Farmer Hudson's yard as Lily disappeared into the barn. He wasn't following her in, not right now anyway. Too many cats hung around in there, and he didn't want to connect with that huge horse's hooves. He'd been on the receiving end of a well-placed kick once before.

Worse than that, Leroy remembered the man with the shotgun, and the ear-splitting noise, and the stinging pain in his rear. All because Leroy had been trying to nab one measly old chicken. There were plenty more in the yard.

Dumb chickens, all they did was peck and cluck. They were only meant to be food.

He'd almost caught one about a month ago. Just as he'd been about to grab it, another cackled an alarm and the whole stupid flock had run around clucking like a troop of gossiping monkeys.

That brought old man Hudson out to the yard, gun in hand, firing at Leroy's retreating back end. Embedded under his skin, in a spot impossible to reach, tiny lead balls festered in the surrounding muscle, painful and irritating, especially when he wagged his tail, which was hardly ever. What did he have to wag about?

He eventually figured out how to get to the chickens' eggs. During the wee hours of the morning, right after the missus let the cacklers out in the yard for the day, he slipped into the hen house through the hole he'd chewed in the frayed screen.

Leroy wasn't a hunter. Never had been. Those eggs had been the difference between starving to death and living.

Now his primary concern centered on the infection burning and throbbing in his tail region. Because of it, he wasn't his usual, quick-thinking self. That had to be the only reason that annoying pup had bested him in the woods and gotten away from him right now.

Keeping an eye on the screen door to the house, Leroy hunkered down at the edge of the yard and waited. Cicadas clicked and chirped in the afternoon heat. Flies swarmed around his head, flew into his eyes, and buzzed around his sore rump.

He grew drowsier by the minute. When was the last time he'd had a good sleep? His stomach grumbled. His wound throbbed, and some lame dog was aggravating the dickens out of him.

If it weren't for that foolish puppy, Leroy could have put an end to the cat he'd treed in the woods.

He couldn't wait to get his teeth into Clawed again. That black fur-ball didn't seem to know the first thing about survival. Couch potato more'n likely. And yet, he'd gotten away.

Leroy didn't know who he hated more, the cat or the puppy. His rear end hurt something awful. He was thirsty and hadn't found any eggs that morning. The hole in the screen had been covered with a board.

There was never any dog food scattered around like when Max used to feed Leroy in their yard.

He missed home even though his memories of life at the trailer grew dimmer every day.

For days after the fire, Leroy had returned to the property that had burned to the ground. He sniffed around the old Chevy he'd regularly napped under. The heat from the fire had melted the tires, and the belly of the car now hugged the ground. He couldn't get under it to sleep anymore.

He scoured the area near the clothesline where Marcy hung sheets he tugged off into the dirt and foraged around the pit where Max dumped the trash Leroy rummaged through for snacks.

Barely detecting his own scent anywhere on the property, he sneezed several times when ash clogged his nose.

He licked the charred spigot that used to drip constantly, keeping his bucket filled.

He tried to swallow, but dehydration stuck his tongue to the roof of his mouth.

No scent of his old companions remained on the property, and no one ever returned.

Leroy almost whined but caught himself. Cats and puppies were crybabies. Not Leroy. Yawning, he just wanted to sleep. He blinked once at the bright sun and rested his head between his front paws.

What was he doing here? No doubt Clawed had gotten out of the tree.

Once more, he glanced at Farmer Hudson's front porch before turning to inspect the open door to the barn. Gosh, he missed his spot on the lumpy, old over-stuffed couch. Everything was that Halloween cat's fault.

And now the irritating puppy who'd helped that cat was hiding in the barn. If only he could get his teeth on her, he'd teach her a lesson or two.

Chapter 17

I, Clawed, was a bit surprised…

… Lily didn't come home that night. Sage kept going to the door and calling, "Lily. Come on, girl." She whistled, waited, called again, and finally came back inside. A few minutes later, Ben went out and did the same. After a while, he got in the car and left to search the neighborhood. Lily wasn't with him when he returned.

"We can't leave her out there," Sage said.

I'd never heard her whine like that.

"We can't drive around all night looking, either," Ben said. "I'm not chasing after her. Put a message up on the Neighborhood Watch website."

That seemed cold-hearted, but the vet had told them not to chase her. Otherwise she'd think it was a game and might run even farther.

Lily was on her own.

She didn't come back that night …

… or the next day.

"Where do you suppose she is?" Tabbert asked me later that afternoon.

He'd woken me from a nap. I'd dragged my bandaged leg to the top of my cat tower and fallen asleep there. But, as most cats are, I'm a light sleeper and the scritch-scratch of his five-toed feet running across the screen pierced my slumber.

I yawned. "I don't know. She's obviously a runner. I mean, that's how she got hit by a car in the first place, by running off." The thought immediately sobered me. That pup who had gotten under all our skins had survived being hit by a car. I hoped I'd never experience that. She was lucky to be alive.

Clearly agitated, Tabbert spun in a circle. "Do you think that's what happened?"

"Well, I sure hope not."

"We should go look for her."

I glanced at my bandaged leg. I still wanted to sleep half the time. The confrontation in the woods with Leroy had taken a lot out of me, or maybe it was the medicine Sage crushed up in my food. She probably thought she was disguising it. It was a bitter pill. I could taste the little grainy pieces. I ate them anyway. I knew what was good for me.

Maybe I could make it out the cat door, but I didn't think I was going to be able to navigate the fence yet, even if Lily had practically flown over it like a bird.

Tabbert pressed me. "What do you think?"

"Not much I can do with this bum leg. Sage and Ben have been looking for her. As a matter of fact, they're out right now."

"Are they looking in the woods?"

I shook my head. "Ben took the car. Sage is walking the neighborhood."

"Come on, then."

I didn't feel like it. A dulling lethargy had overtaken me, and I could barely deal with it.

"What is wrong with you?" Tabbert demanded.

"Nothing. I'm just not sure I can get over the fence."

"You won't know until you give it a try."

Tabbert could be really annoying. This was one of those times. It wasn't that I didn't care what happened to Lily. I'd even come to like the energetic dudette.

Speaking of energy, I didn't have any. The cast felt like a lead sinker tied to my leg. My body dragged like I hadn't slept in a hundred years. A sudden thought of Gidget overwhelmed me so badly that I had to gulp a painful knot in my throat several times before I finally swallowed it. Was I ever going to see her again?

A mosquito buzzed between my eyes and flew in circles around my head. "Lily helped you. Get your sorry self out there and help my friend or I swear I'll stay in your ear and buzz you crazy."

Skeeter. Annoying. And behind her, my friend Tabbert nodding like he was agreeing with her. Traitor.

"And what am I supposed to do with this?" Exaggerating weakness, I waved my mangled back limb in the air.

"She had a broken leg, too." Skeeter's buzz grew louder in my ear. "And stitches and a broken pelvis, and they removed the top of her femur. She climbed over that fence like a prize winner of the Westminster Kennel Club just to come to find you. Any more excuses?"

What could I say? Outnumbered, I climbed down off my tower and limped to the cat door. I hesitated.

"What? Are you chicken?"

I dug in my ear. If I could just catch hold of a piece of Skeeter, I'd yank her buzzing tongue out, but I couldn't get at her.

I pushed my nose through the cat door. Tabbert was waiting in the middle of the walkway outside. Didn't they understand? Leroy had broken my leg, bitten me. What if he was out there?

My conscience got the better of me.

My hurt leg got hung up on the door as I leaped out. I'd just have to work harder to hold it up. I had to stop my stinking thinking and get on with the mission. We had to find Lily.

Otherwise that infernal mosquito was going to buzz in my ear for the rest of my life.

Chapter 18

They say if you don't use it...

...you lose it. It had been several weeks since I'd been able to romp outside. I rolled over onto my back and stretched out in the grass. The sun warmed my sore leg. It would've been nice to soak up the rays for a while.

Skeeter dive bombed me.

Tabbert clung to my ear. "Come on, Clawed."

I approached the chain link fence. I doubted I could make it to the top, let alone land on the other side without further injuring myself.

"You can do this."

Tabbert probably thought he was encouraging me, but his repetitive nagging only annoyed me.

After half a dozen tries, I finally scaled the fence. In my efforts, the bandage on my leg ripped some and now trailed behind me. Barely able to keep up, I was out of breath by the time we reached the edge of the yard.

Remembering what my last escapade had cost me, I quickly looked back over my shoulder. The house seemed a long distance away. If Leroy came out of the woods right now, I wasn't sure I'd be able to make it back to safety.

"Come on!" Tinged with a sense of urgency, Tabbert's voice forced me to look away from the protection of home. I wanted to be mad at that pipsqueak lizard. Ever since I'd met him, there'd been nothing but chaos in my life. The minute I thought that, I felt bad.

Pushing away visions of a full food dish and the comfy couch, I followed Tabbert as best I could. Maybe I'd just hate that annoying Skeeter instead.

We passed the pond and headed for the woods. For a moment, my heart wrenched. Tikky had tried to save Gidget from falling into that sinkhole before the artesian spring and a week of torrential rains had filled it in.

I still found it hard to believe Gidget was a glassy Blingling instead of a real-live furry feline. It was dark the night Lily had saved me from Leroy. Even with my great night vision, I hadn't seen Gidget during the long walk home. I'd only heard her voice. Had I been dreaming, or was being practically invisible a Blingling anomaly?

Skeeter hummed around my head. "Get a move on."

"Buzz off." My leg ached.

When we reached the clearing in the woods, we stopped to rest.

"We need a plan," Tabbert said.

"Whatever it is, we also need to keep an eye out for Leroy. We're looking for Lily, not a fight with the mange."

"I've got that covered." Skeeter flew in circles around my head. "I'm known as 'Triple Threat.'"

Oh brother, no conceit in Skeeter's family.

"Really?" Tabbert spun in a circle like a dog chasing its tail.

"Really. I use visual, olfactory, and thermal cues to hone in on my targets. I can detect carbon dioxide that humans and animals exhale."

I needed a nap. "Are we looking for Lily, or are we having a science lesson?"

Skeeter ignored me. "I'll fly ahead and check it out. My thermal senses detect body heat, so if anything's there, whatever or whoever it is will be easy to find. Then, I'll come back and report."

"What are we supposed to do in the meantime?"

"Use your own skills."

I bit my tongue to keep from saying something nasty. Tabbert had been right about one thing. Crabby to the marrow in my bones, nothing felt good right now.

I wanted to go home and be near Bling. Hopefully, someday real soon, I'd get to spend more time with Gidget—even if she was a shiny, faceted critter with beady black eyes now.

As vulnerable as a blind, newborn kitten, I limped into the bushes while Tabbert scooted after Skeeter who flew above the ground just ahead of him.

Let them run. My leg throbbed and my butt muscles, overworked from favoring my injured leg, felt like they were on fire. I hunkered down under a saw palmetto to rest and wait. Skeeter wasn't the only one with special skills.

I could sit perfectly still without blinking for a long time. My dim-light vision was excellent. My whiskers helped me detect things around me even in the darkest of night. My sense of smell was about fourteen times better than a human's.

Sheesh, now I was giving myself a science lesson.

"Hey there."

Could this day get any worse? "I thought I smelled something rotten."

"Nice to see you, too," Tikky said. "What are you doing out here?"

"None of your business." I wasn't about to tell him I was searching for the pup. If I admitted I was concerned about her, I'd lose face, not that I was worried about what he thought.

He wasn't fooled easily. "I just saw your reptile buddy running through the orange grove. You two just hanging out? Or have you decided to get off your comfy couch and exercise your bum leg?"

I sighed. "If you must know, we're looking for Lily. She lost her mind over a squirrel, climbed the fence, and hasn't been home since yesterday morning."

"I know where she is."

"You do?"

Tikky nodded. "In Farmer Hudson's barn. She ran in there yesterday."

"You're friends with those cats. How about you go get her and show her the way home?"

"Why don't you?"

"Man, my leg is killing me."

"That scamp won't follow me. She doesn't know me, and this isn't the time for training a puppy. You've got to introduce us formal-like first. Anyway, I don't see why I should care anyway. Last time I made friends with one of your friends, she died."

"Gidget's not dead!" If I wasn't so darned sore, I'd have been on him like flies eating rotten meat.

"Oh yeah, she's a Blingling. That's a good one. You're all losing your minds. First the reptile." He smirked. "Well, I can understand that. But you. I guess that's what comes from being a couch potato."

My bad mood darkened, and my claws came out.

Tikky backed away. "Don't go getting your tail in a twist. Come on. Follow me. By the way," he said over his shoulder as we made our way through the orange grove to Farmer Hudson's property, "Leroy's hanging around over there today."

I had all I could do to keep from turning around and running home, but I wasn't about to let that pompous ball of fluff think I was afraid.

Was that it? Was I afraid?

You ever been bit by a dog? Not fun.

Chapter 19

Sleep doesn't come easily...

...when hunger gnaws at your stomach.

Groggy with exhaustion, Lily opened her eyes to the dimming light of evening descending upon Farmer Hudson's barn.

She remained hidden in the hay when a tall man wearing a wide-brimmed straw hat came in and set a large dented pan on the floor.

"Suppertime."

Lily's instincts told her to stay put even though hunger told her otherwise. Kittens appeared from under carts. Cats leapt down from the loft, and the big white horse huffed and snuffled and stomped on the wide plank floor.

"One of these days, I've got to round up some of these kittens, Nel. Barn's getting overrun with them again."

"That's just so wrong." Nel tossed her head and snorted.

The man patted her on the neck.

Just like Clawed had said. Humans didn't understand animal talk.

Lily longed to be home with Clawed. She'd never seen so many cats in her life. And that horse. Huge.

Hunger got the best of her after the man left. How was she going to get past that barb-clawed crowd?

"Finally woke up, did you?" Nel's warm snuffling nose plunged into Lily's face.

Lily rolled over onto her back, her belly exposed. "Friends?" She whined.

"That's right." Nel nodded. "Friends." Looking around the room, she glared at every cat. "Move over and let her get a few bites. There's plenty."

She turned back to Lily. "Come on now."

Lily slunk on her belly toward the food pan. A white male swiped at her.

A red tabby hissed in her face. "Don't gobble it all up."

"I won't."

Nel stood over the dish in a protective stance, but whether it was for her or the cats, Lily wasn't sure. She lapped up a few mouthfuls of crunchies and quickly backed away.

After everyone had eaten and settled down at a cautious distance, Nel asked, "Where you from?"

"Sage and Ben's house."

"Sure. We've heard of them, nice people. So, you'll be going home then?"

Lily glanced at the open barn door.

Nel followed her gaze. "What's out there?"

"A hurt dog. His name's Leroy, and he's mean. Chased me in here. He broke Clawed's leg too. I tried to tell him Sage and Ben could help, but he just got mad and chased me."

Nel snuffed Lily's face. "What were you doing out there?"

"Well ... I ... uh, was chasing a squirrel."

Nel nodded and grinned. "Who's Clawed?"

By the time Lily finished the telling, several cats had come closer.

"Sounds like you've gotten around Leroy a few times now," Nel said. "You can do it again."

Lily shook her head. "I don't know."

"I can take you to the corn field." Nel's head bobbed up and down rapidly, as if she were eager to get going. "Then you can scoot home from there. It can't be that far. How long were you running?"

"Forever!"

Outside the open barn doors, a setting sun blazed behind a stand of pines that studded the distant horizon.

Lily whined, "Can't I stay here for the night?"

Nel shook her head. "Your people will worry. Didn't you say that when Clawed got hurt and didn't come home, they went out looking for him?"

"And when they come find me, I'll go home with them." Lily smiled, raised her eyebrows, and thumped her tail on the barn floor.

"Silly pup. Go lie down."

Chapter 20

Leroy snuck around…

…behind Farmer Hudson's house. He slipped past the rain barrel, ducked under the wagon, and came out under the other side in front of the chicken coop. The sun was disappearing fast. If he wanted an egg, he'd better get it before the chickens came in to roost for the night.

A board covered the torn screen where he usually pushed through to steal a meal. He dug at the perimeter of the coop. He'd get at those chickens one way or the other. Maybe while he was at it, that scamp of a pup might get a notion to come out of the barn and head home. Leroy would be right there to escort her to the woods, by the scruff of her neck if necessary. He had a score to settle with her.

Leroy took a minute to rest. His nose was dry. His ears were on fire. Sizzling bolts of pain shot through his backside every time he sat down.

"Lily disappears last night, and now Clawed hasn't come home." Ben wrung his hands. "I knew I shouldn't have installed that cat door. What's going on?"

"I don't know. Remember the night Clawed came home hurt? I think Lily helped him. Maybe Clawed went to find Lily. We'd better go looking," Sage said. "Hopefully they'll be together."

Ben shook his head. "With their black fur, we'll never find them in the dark."

"And neither one of us will get a good night's sleep if we don't at least try."

Chapter 21

Tabbert...

...quickly scooted ahead. "Come on Clawed. What's taking you so long?"

"My bandage got caught in the brush. I had to tear it off." Being free of the bandage made me feel stronger, unencumbered, like I was really healed.

I caught up with Tabbert. We followed close behind Tikky, my sensitive whiskers detecting every branch, blade of grass, and wisp of breeze. The fur on my back rose when I caught a rancid odor—Leroy and another familiar scent when we reached the edge of Farmer Hudson's yard–Lily.

There was no turning back now.

Fear cramped my belly. I wished I were back at the house watching *Wheel of Fortune* with Ben.

"What now?" Tikky whispered.

"You tell me," I said. "You're the one who knows all about this place."

"I don't have a plan. I was just being nice and helping you find Lily. She's your new pet, not mine."

"Nice," I said with a deliberate sting of sarcasm.

"Since when do you care?"

"Since now." I faced him and growled.

Tikky puffed up his chest, squared his shoulders, and glared at me.

We had too many other things to handle to get into it just then. My leg ached, and I was on a mission to find a puppy, not get into it with Tikky.

"I'll tear you up later if you want; but right now, let's focus."

Tikky shrugged. "Anything you say, Clawedykins."

I growled and bit my tongue."

When we reached the edge of Farmer Hudson's barnyard, we hunkered down in the bushes to consider a plan.

Chapter 22

Fighting rarely solves anything…

… but sometimes stuff happens. Especially if you're hungry, lonely, angry, or tired. Or ill.

Leroy barfed twice and then again. Egg shells scratched his throat as he expelled the contents of his stomach onto the ground. Eating hadn't helped him feel any better. Why did every day have to be such a struggle?

Of all the times Leroy had watched the goings-on in the barn, today he wished he was in there eating some of that food Farmer Hudson brought every day for those yowling, rake-clawed barn cats. Seemed like enough food for everyone.

His attention was drawn to the ear-grating screech of squealing brakes. Squinting against the glare of oncoming headlights, Leroy crouched down in the scrub at the edge of the yard. An old truck pulled into the driveway. An unkempt, bearded man stepped out. There was something familiar about him.

Farmer Hudson stepped out onto his porch and leaned a shotgun against the screen door frame.

Max yelled across the yard. "How's y'all?"

"What do you want?" Farmer Hudson said.

"Looking for my dog. You seen him?"

"You mean that mutt that used to hang around that junkyard you called home?"

"I ain't there no more," Max said. "I run him off when the place burned down. Couldn't take him with me. Had no place to go. Been back a couple times to find him. Ain't seen him though."

The farmer shook his head. "Only thing 'round here is a chicken thief. And if I see him again, I'm going to shoot him."

Overhead, the night sky glittered.

Leroy's stomach churned. The egg he'd eaten earlier hadn't been enough to fill him, especially since he'd upchucked most of that. He wanted to lie at someone's feet, be used as a foot rest, let someone scratch the back of his ears.

Staying in the shadows, Leroy moved toward the truck. The visitor's voice drew him closer to the porch. Pretty sure that it was his old friend, Max, he eyed the gun leaning against the door frame.

He inched forward, his bony shoulders hunched, every whisker sensitive to any sign of threat. His backside ached. His stomach growled. He longed for the comfort that only a friend could give. Longing fed his bravery, familiarity swept away his caution.

A snarling shadow loomed over him a split second before it landed on top of him and pinned him to the ground.

Farmer Hudson's chocolate lab sank his teeth into the scruff of fur behind Leroy's right ear.

"Yow!" Leroy bit into the lab's double coat, clamped onto nothing. The big dog overpowered Leroy and pinned him to the ground.

Through his long months in the woods, Leroy had lost weight. On his best day, he'd never weighed much, and even though he was hungry and weak with fever, he wasn't without a few junkyard tricks. He played dead and let his body go limp.

"Butch!" Farmer Hudson called from the porch.

The larger dog released his grip.

Still on his back, Leroy snarled and lunged for Butch's throat. He dug at the lab's chest with long-neglected nails that raked through the lab's thick fur and scored the skin underneath.

Butch jumped away. Leroy rolled onto his feet. Teeth bared, the dogs faced each other growling. Butch sprang. Leroy ducked and rolled. When Butch came back at him, Leroy leaped onto the bigger dog's side and chomped on his ear. Butch howled and rolled over.

A thundering explosion broke up the fight. Butch dashed to the porch and stood, muscles quivering, by Farmer Hudson's side.

Leroy ran.

Max cackled. "Looked like that mutt was about to take down that fancy dog of yours."

"That your dog?"

"Looked a lot smaller than my dog. Couldn't see him too good in the dark.

Farmer Hudson stepped down off the porch. "If this one isn't yours, I guess you won't mind if I shoot it. He's a thief, and he better not come around no more. Next time I might not miss."

Max walked around his truck. "Where'd he go?"

"Better for him if he run off."

Max shook his head. "You didn't have to shoot at him. I'll be back tomorrow, see if I can find him."

Chapter 23

An earth-shattering boom …

…startled Lily from a nap. Kittens scattered to every corner of the barn. Nel and a dozen whiskered felines tiptoed to the door and peered out.

Lily crept up behind them just in time to see Leroy barreling toward the open barn door.

Nel tossed her head and jumped out of the way. Hissing cats leaped on top of hay bales, under wheelbarrows, and over Lily's back, when Leroy barged in.

He stopped briefly, his eyes darting around the room before he dashed into the shadows in a dark corner where a rusty tractor was parked. He dropped down and pulled himself under it.

"That's him," Lily said.

Nel cocked an eyebrow. "Him who?"

"That's Leroy, the one I was running from, the one who chomped on Clawed's leg and broke it. Tabbert came and got me. I tried to help, but I chased a squirrel...."

"Whoa there. Slow down, Runabout. You say his name is Leroy?"

Lily nodded and whined as cats gathered close to Big Nel's protective hooves. "Yup. And he's sick."

"How do you know?"

"When I was lost in the orange grove, I heard him whining and went to investigate. His back end is swollen and looks like some gooey stuff all over his fur. Smells bad, too."

Nel nodded. "No wonder."

"What do you mean?"

"He's been killing our chickens and stealing their eggs. Farmer Hudson doesn't take kindly to that. I suspect Hudson's only trying to scare him off by shooting over his head. Some of the buckshot must've hit him."

"He's probably hungry."

Nel nodded. "I'm sure he is, but that doesn't give him the right to steal."

"We think he's homeless."

"Hm, who's 'we?'"

"Me and Clawed and Tabbert. Skeeter too." Lily explained who they all were, how she'd come to know them, and how she'd been taken in by Sage and Ben after she'd been hit by a car.

"You really are a runabout, aren't you?"

Lily looked up at the horse towering over her. "I don't mean to be."

"I wanted to tell him he should follow me home. Sage and Ben would help just like they helped me. He didn't give me a chance to talk. He just chased me. That's how I ended up here."

Nel stretched her long neck toward the trembling puppy. "Well, ever since you arrived yesterday, we've been wondering what to do with you. Now, I'm thinking you're here so you can help us figure out what to do with him."

Lily, Big Nel, and the barn cats looked in the direction of the ancient tractor.

Chapter 24

No, you don't know what it's like…

… when nothing feels all right. Starving, hurting, and more miserable than he'd been in his entire life, Leroy glared at dozens of eyes that peered under the tractor. He'd have growled and bared his teeth if he'd had one ounce of energy left.

He shouldn't have run into the barn. Farmer Hudson had made it clear Leroy wasn't welcome. There was nowhere else to go. He couldn't spend one more lonely night in the woods. Why hadn't Max helped him?

He wanted to sleep for a gazillion years, but he wasn't about to take his eyes off the army of critters standing around the tractor. The fight in him was gone but his fear of being hurt wasn't.

If only he could close his eyes for just a minute.

"Hey, Leroy."

Leroy didn't answer.

"I know you're awake," Lily said. "Your eyes are open."

Leroy shifted farther back into the shadows. He whined when his rump nudged up against a rear tire. "Go away."

"You're hurt."

"It's none of your business."

"I know what it's like to hurt. I got hit by a car. My leg was in a cast forever. I had stitches."

"Tough luck, kid."

"I know someone who can help."

"Don't want help."

"Sure you do. You could come home with me."

"I'm not going anywhere with you."

"Doesn't look like you can stay here."

"Why don't you leave me alone and let me sleep?" Leroy closed his eyes and didn't open them again.

Chapter 25

We'd all seen Farmer Hudson take a shot at Leroy...

...before the mangy mutt ran into the barn where Tikky said Lily was.

Tabbert whispered. "Hey, Clawed. What are we going to do now?"

"I don't know."

"What do you think is going on in there?"

"Hush."

Tabbert clung to my ear. "I don't want to stay out here all night."

"We've got to get that thick-headed pup."

"How're you planning on doing that?"

"I'm not planning anything. Tikky's going in there. He knows all about this place."

"Wait a minute." Tikky puffed out his chest. "I didn't say that."

"Yes, you did," I said. "You told me you come here and eat. Go in and talk to those cats. Find that rascal, and we'll take her home."

"What about Leroy?"

"Just sneak in, find Lily, and bring her out."

Tikky sighed. "Sheesh. Why'd I bother coming with you?"

"Because that's what friends do," Tabbert said.

"What if Leroy sees me?"

"You're the tough guy," I said. "You can handle him, can't you?"

"That puppy is your friend. Either you come with me, or I'm not going in."

Tikky and I stared into each other's eyes. For once Tabbert remained quiet, probably scared speechless.

I didn't want to think about how afraid I was.

The last rays of daylight disappeared as Tabbert and I followed Tikky between two loose boards on the back wall of the barn.

 Once inside, my eyes quickly adjusted to more dark.

"Wait here," Tikky said. "I'll talk to Nel."

I'd come this far. The time for waiting was over.

I wished the voice in my head would be quiet. It almost always led me to trouble. Even though every instinct screamed "No!" I couldn't stay behind. I stayed on Tikky's heels as he approached a huge, white behemoth standing in the center of the room near a scrambled mound of hay.

"Hey, Nel."

The horse swung around in our direction. "Hey, Tikky. You hungry? You're a little late. I see you brought a friend."

I'd never seen a horse up close before. TV didn't do them justice. I couldn't help but cringe.

I glanced at the empty galvanized pan and might have licked my chops but for a rank odor that permeated the air.

"This is Clawed."

Nel tossed her huge head. "Heard the name. You looking for a black puppy? She thought her people would come to get her. You and her friends?"

Tikky shook his head. "She saved Clawed, and I got roped into helping return the favor. Where's she at?"

"Snuggled up in there." Nel gestured to a pile of hay. "Hold on a sec before you wake her up. What about Leroy?"

Tikky looked over both shoulders, swung a full 180°, and stepped closer to the big horse's hooves. "Where is he?"

In a million years, no one could have told me I'd follow Tikky under the belly of a massive horse. My insides were churning so badly I thought I was having a heart attack.

"Over there, under the tractor."

Tikky peered into the dark. "I don't see anything."

"Smell anything?"

"Something rotten."

"That's him."

"Not our problem," Tikky said. "We've come to get the puppy. That's all."

Nel stomped the floor. "Leroy is everybody's problem."

Wanting to jump out of my fur, I didn't know which way to turn without getting slammed by one of those hooves.

Nel lowered her head and looked me in the eyes. "Come out from under there. I hear Leroy broke your leg."

"Yes."

"Is it better?"

"Sort of."

"Someone helped you?"

Tikky interrupted. "What's your point?"

Nel touched her nose to mine and huffed warm air in my face. "Why did you risk coming through the woods again, after being hurt and all?"

"I came to find Lily."

"Leroy needs help."

"I don't see how that makes rot mutt our problem," Tikky said.

(I loved Tikky for saying that.)

"He's hurt. Lily tried talking him into following her home, but he refused."

Tikky shrugged. "There you go. You can lead a horse to water...."

"If Old Man Hudson finds him in here, he'll shoot him."

"And we should care ...because?"

Nel snorted. "It could happen to any one of us. Hudson doesn't like too many stray cats hanging around. What if he shot you and you needed help?"

My courage slowly returned as I listened to Nel's gentle voice. "I'm not a stray."

"That's my point. Neither was Leroy. I'm pretty sure he had a home. Leroy doesn't know any more about taking care of himself in the woods than you do. What if he's afraid?"

I glanced around the room. Dozens of eyes blinked and sparkled in the rising moonlight. I'd had enough. I hissed in Nel's face. "I really don't see how we're going to get him to change his mind."

"Talk to him," Nel said.

"How do I know you're not just trying to get rid of him?"

"I am. You must have been outside and seen what happened. Did Hudson shoot at him again? Leroy can't stay here."

I sighed. Instead of this being a rescue mission to find Lily, it sounded like it was turning into a rescue mission for Leroy. Had everyone forgotten what that dog had done to me? "I'm waking up that runaway puppy. She started this mess by running off."

With Tabbert still clinging to my forehead, I limped across the barn floor and pounced into the mound of hay where Nel had indicated Lily was sleeping. "Get up, troublemaker."

Chapter 26

Tikky, a horse, and a pile of cats ...

...surrounded us. Skeeter buzzed around my head.

Lily barked. "Can we go home now?"

"Hold on there, runabout." Nel snorted and swished her tail. "We need to decide what to do about Leroy. Nobody's going anywhere until we do."

Lily shook hay from her fur. "He can come home with us. Sage and Ben would get him fixed up."

"No way!" I meowed. "He broke my leg and just about killed me."

"I know. But, that's because he doesn't feel good," Lily said.

The animals gathered around stared at me as if expecting me to accept this insane idea.

Tabbert whispered in my ear, "Remember how grouchy you were when you weren't feeling good."

I'd already come to terms with having a puppy in the house. There was no room for another dog, especially a mean one. "Are you turning on me now? It was all that dog's fault."

"That dog has a name," Nel said.

"So do I, and I'm going home."

On my way out through the loose boards, as I passed the tractor, I hissed. A low growl came from beneath it. I took off running and hoped Leroy stayed in the barn.

Tabbert rode atop my head. I didn't hear a squeak out of him. The voice in my head was talking too loudly.

Lily looked up at Nel. "What do we do now?"

"Just exactly what we were planning to do, talk Leroy into following you home."

Lily sat back. "That's crazy. I don't know the way, and now that Clawed's gone...."

"I do," Skeeter buzzed.

"There you go," Nel said. "Come on. We've got to fix this, now."

Lily looked out the barn door in the direction Clawed had taken. Wispy clouds scudded across the face of the moon. An owl hooted. "What if he comes after me?"

"You see these hooves? I won't let Leroy anywhere near you until I think it's safe."

"I don't want to," Lily whined.

"Then why are you still here?"

Lily looked back and forth from the open door to Nel. Her muscles quivered. Her eyes sparkled. "Sage and Ben can help him," she said quietly.

"Then we'd better get to it." Nel turned and headed into the barn.

"Wait." Lily stood, her tail straight in the air. "Wait!" she panted nervously. "What do I say? How do I do this?"

Nel blew a warm breath in her face. "Just be yourself."

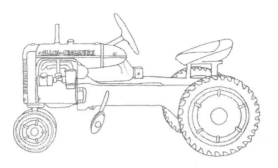

Chapter 27

Leroy opened his eyes...

...when someone called his name. Max? Every muscle ached. His tongue was dry, his breathing labored. He blinked to clear his blurred vision. He could barely lift his head.

Beyond the front of the tractor someone called his name again.

"Leroy? You okay?"

Leroy growled. The pup, and the only way out was straight at her and through the horse's legs. He didn't have the energy.

"Are you okay?"

"Stay away from me."

"Nope."

Leroy growled.

Lily looked up. Nel's belly loomed over her head. The four white legs surrounding her did little to curb her fear.

Nel tossed her mane and snorted. "You can do this."

Lily dropped onto her belly and peered under the tractor. "I'm not leaving unless you come with me."

His muzzle resting on his paws, Leroy shook his head.

"Don't say no. You can't stay here."

"I don't need you feeling sorry for me."

"We all heard the shot. You can't steal anymore of Farmer Hudson's chickens. If he catches you, you're done for."

"I don't care."

Nel snuffed and kicked the tire. "Come out from under there."

Lily wriggled under the tractor.

Leroy whined. He was so tired. For just a minute he'd close his eyes, for just a minute.

He drifted into something warm, something like an overstuffed couch with lumpy cushions.

Chapter 28

In the orange grove…

…I stopped in a patch of deer grass. My leg was sore. I hadn't walked this much since Leroy.… I couldn't think about that anymore.

Tabbert dangled upside down between my eyes. "What are we stopping for?"

"I'm taking a rest."

Tabbert's dewlap flared. "Taking a rest? Let's get home. I don't like being out at night. Aren't you the least bit worried about Leroy coming after us? And the woods could be full of evil dogs and cats—oops, no offense. I wonder if Tikky's out there."

"Will you be quiet?" Miffed because he'd stuck up for Leroy instead of me, I thought about swiping him off my head, but I could tell he was upset, so I didn't.

Well, anyway, I wouldn't.

I, too, wondered if Tikky was close by.

He would be a big help if Leroy showed up. Confused, I mulled over the events of the day. I could have stayed at home and relied on my people to do what they do best. Take care of us.

Instead, at Tabbert's urging, and at great peril to myself, I'd gone searching for a puppy who, months earlier, had rescued me. And yet, here I was, walking in the dark and hadn't done a thing to bring her home. Hmph. She'd had her chance.

I slowly picked my way through the woods, hoping, once I got home, I'd finally be able to get a good night's sleep.

"Clawed?"

I recognized the voice and stopped, my heart thudding in my chest.

"It's Gidget!" Tabbert slid off my back and skittered away as if seconds ago he hadn't told me he didn't like being out in the dark.

"Gidget? Where are you?" I asked.

"I'm here."

A sparkle and two beady eyes gleamed up at me from between my front feet. I could have stepped on her. "Gidget." I crouched down onto my belly and gazed into her tiny eyes. "What are you doing here?"

"I came to keep you company."

"How'd you know where I was?"

"Stocker told me."

"That dude knows everything, doesn't he?"

"Seems so."

"How'd you get here?"

"Stocker and I came together."

A gleaming stag, much larger than Gidget but barely coming up to my elbow, stepped up beside her. "Hello, Clawed. I'm pleased to finally meet you."

"Yes. Yes..." I stuttered and nodded and kept nodding. I must have looked like a bobbing duck. "Likewise."

As quickly as he had gone, Tabbert reappeared. He spun in a circle. "I couldn't find Gidget. Did you see her? Did you talk to her?"

"Settle down, Tabbert. She's right here by me."

"Gidget! Oh gosh. That's Stocker. Uh ... hey, sir, uh ... hello, Stocker."

"Hello, Tabbert. Where are you two headed?"

"Home," I said, deliberately adding a sting of defiance to my tone.

Stocker looked left and right. "Where's Lily? Gidget mentioned that you were out here to find her."

"She stayed behind," Tabbert said. "She wanted Leroy to come with us so Sage and Ben could help him get better."

"Really?" Stocker looked directly at me.

I bit my tongue even though I wanted to tell him to mind his own business. All day long, everyone had been telling me what to do, where to go, and what I should think.

Tabbert stood at my feet with Gidget and Stocker. He suddenly seemed so small. I couldn't remember any time he hadn't seemed bigger than life. I felt like they were all ganging up on me.

First, I'd lost Gidget to a strange place in the garden called Bling. Now my only best friend left in my world was betraying me for the second time in one day.

Stocker nodded, his well-branched rack glistening in the moonlight. "I see." He looked up at me. "I can certainly understand why you would be against that, Clawed."

"Don't patronize me." This was turning into a long night. I wanted to get home. Instead, I sat back on my haunches and did my best to glare. "Why should it matter to you?" I asked. "Who are you anyway? And why is Gidget living out there in the garden instead of at home with us where she belongs?"

"Gidget is right where she's supposed to be, Clawed. If not for me, she wouldn't be alive. I'm sure Tabbert has told you I'm the ruler of Bling. When you reach your tenth life, like she did, hopefully you'll come there too.

"Why would I want to?"

"Because you'd be with Gidget. That's what you've been wanting, isn't it?"

"Do you know everything that's my head?"

"I am you, Clawed."

"Me?"

"I'm your conscience, the voice of reason and forgiveness. I'm the best of everything you are." Stocker pranced back and forth. A bright gleam reflected off his shiny antlers momentarily blinding me.

"Lily helped save you, and because of that you came out here to help her. You're not feeling so good right now because you've left her behind, and why? Fear. I don't blame you for that. You've suffered plenty at the teeth of that dog.

"Lily's had a few slams herself. Everyone does. Look at Gidget. Nine lives, and now she's on her tenth. You've got a few more to go yet."

"Are you and Gidget and all of Bling in some kind of magic world?"

"You could say that."

I stared down at the strange glassy creature who had once been one of my best friends. Gidget, the yowling, snippy cat who used to put me in my place, had been reduced to a tiny, beady-eyed talking crystal.

"She's much more than that, Clawed," Stocker said.

"Is there no privacy? You have no right to read my mind all the time. Do you know everything I think?"

"I know you're wishing I'd get lost. I'm not telling you what to do, Clawed. You can go home, but there's a part of you that disagrees. It's entirely up to you what you do next."

Guilt trip. I tried to shield my mind, block my thoughts; but visions of the barn, and Lily, and Leroy crowded my brain.

"You're the *Jeopardy* expert, Clawed. Who said, 'You have nothing to fear but fear itself?'"

That was an easy one. I assumed Stocker already knew it was Franklin D. Roosevelt. He seemed to know everything else.

"Having courage doesn't mean you're not afraid, Clawed. It means, despite your fear, you're willing to face something that frightens you."

"Easier said than done." Hearing myself say it, I suddenly imploded. My breath caught in my throat. My heart thudded in my chest so strongly I thought it would burst.

Tikky was wrong. I wasn't a spoiled, couch potato. I'd been wallowing in a pity party, and I was one big, fat scaredy-cat. Petrified of Leroy, scared of what Gidget had become, afraid of change. I had allowed fear to paralyze my thoughts and actions ever since Gidget had ... disappeared? Died?

One minute she'd been an ordinary cat like me, by my side in everything. The next she was this strange, glassy creature. I wasn't even sure I still knew her. I loved her and missed her, but I didn't want to be like her. If Leroy got me, what would I become?

"Facing that truth is half the battle, Clawed."

Oh, how I wished he'd go away and leave me alone. My leg throbbed. I was so tired I couldn't see straight.

Tabbert climbed up my leg and hung over my ear. "Whatever you decide, Clawed. I'm with you."

"So am I," Gidget said.

"As am I," said Stocker.

I expelled a long breath, releasing every thread of tension, frustration, and irritation I'd been harboring. I didn't want to think anymore. I had to go back and get Lily. As much as I'd rather be safe and sound at home watching TV or taking a catnap on my tower, it was time I stood up for a new friend. What would be would be.

"Come on." I turned and headed back through the orange grove to Farmer Hudson's barnyard as the first glimmering rays of dawn brightened the sky.

Chapter 29

Leroy awoke to the sound of a truck...

... pulling into Farmer Hudson's yard. The puppy snored by his side. A soft growl escaped his throat. Lily looked up, rolled onto her side, and whined.

"Get out of my way or I'll eat you," he whispered.

Lily stayed on her back while Leroy crawled out from under the tractor.

Nel kept the cats corralled in the other corner by the hay.

Leroy headed for the open barn door. Lily followed not too far behind.

Tabbert and I watched from the bushes. I had no idea where Gidget and Stocker were. What could they do anyway? I still had no idea what I was going to do.

A man got of the truck and headed toward the front porch where Farmer Hudson stood with a shotgun in his hands and a larger-than-life dog sitting by his side. The dog's head was almost as big as my whole body.

I shuddered.

Scoping out the yard, I spied Leroy standing in the barn doorway and Lily behind his flank. Where that puppy got her guts was beyond me.

"Morning, Hudson," the man said.

The big dog standing beside Hudson growled.

The farmer placed a hand on the dog's head. "Hush, Butch. What do you want, Max?"

"I told you I'd be back this morning to see if I can find my dog."

"Might be him over yonder." Farmer Hudson lifted the shotgun to his shoulder and aimed toward the barn door.

 Tikky sidled up next to me. "This ought to be interesting."

"Where've you been?" I whispered. I didn't give him a chance to answer. It didn't matter. "Lily's in there." I pointed toward the barn. "See her behind Leroy?"

Tikky stretched his nose through the bushes and squinted. "Well, I'll be. What're we going to do?"

I stood beside him. We looked each other in the eye for a long moment. "Think you can manage that big dog while I take down Farmer Hudson?"

"No problem," Tikky said.

"Sneak back through the bushes by the side yard and catch them by surprise from the side of the porch."

"Let's go."

Without taking another minute to think about it, I took off running. I just barely detected the pinch in my ear where Tabbert must have been hanging on for dear life.

Tikky and I ran neck-and-neck through the bushes, across the grass, up onto the porch. Tikky and I both landed on the big dog's back at the same time. I could tell by the way the dog yelped Tikky had grabbed hold. I didn't. I was after the man with the gun.

I pushed off the dog's back, landed on Farmer Hudson's shoulder, and dug in. He jerked, lost his balance, and tried grabbing me as he fell. The gun went off.

My ears rang. For a moment, it seemed that everything went still, dead still.

As Farmer Hudson scrambled to his feet, I retracted my claws from his shoulder, leaped off the porch, and fled to the barn—right toward my enemy.

I stopped not ten feet from him. Behind him, Nel and a crowd of cats inched their way toward Leroy's back. Tikky stood beside me.

"Leroy, is that you boy?"

I recognized the voice of the same man who'd said he'd come for his dog.

Leroy quickly glanced over my shoulder. "Max!" He didn't back down but continued to glare at me. "You and that ball of fluff standing next to you aren't going to beat me this time. I've got reinforcements now."

"Look behind you. You're surrounded."

"They're scaredy-cats, just like you." He lowered his head and bared his teeth. Slowly, he advanced toward me and Tikky.

"No, wait! That's Clawed." Lily ran around in front of Leroy. "He's here to help."

Leroy growled. Lily rolled over onto her back in front of him.

"I told you before to get out of my way." He growled again and snapped at her.

I snarled and leaped with all my claws extended. I longed to tear his face apart.

Something slammed into my side and sent me flailing through the air. I landed on all four feet by the barn. I shook my head.

Nel neighed and a dozen or more cats hissed. They crowded closer together.

"Go on." Standing over Leroy, Max jabbed a pitchfork at us and booted Lily out of the way. "Get out of here." She tucked her tail under her and ran to Nel.

Tikky yowled just beyond the sharp tines of the fork, his fur puffed out so much he looked three times his normal size. I joined him.

"Max!" Leroy barked.

"Leroy. Come here boy." Max threw the pitchfork at us, knelt, and put his arms around the dirty dog.

Leroy whined, "Max. I thought you left me."

Max scratched behind Leroy's ears, smoothed the fur down along his sides, his hands stopping at Leroy's back end. "It's okay, boy. I'm going to take you home. Come on. I'll get you fixed up."

Tikky and I growling, Leroy still baring his teeth at us, Max led him to the truck, opened the door, and helped Leroy up into the front seat.

Good riddance.

Farmer Hudson called out from the porch. "You'd better take that chicken thief away from here. Next time he shows up, I won't miss."

One split second later, he turned his aim on me and Tikky. A head-splitting boom sent us high-tailing it into the barn. Whistling whooshes sailed over my head. Something stung my ear.

"Clawed!" Lily ran to me, a dozen cats surrounding her. "Tikky!"

"No time to talk," Tikky said. "We've got to get out of here. Nel, bar the door."

Nel tossed her head and whinnied.

"Come on." Tikky ran to the loose boards on the back wall where we'd slipped in earlier in the evening. He went out first.

Home. We were headed home, and Leroy wouldn't be following us. I almost breathed a sigh of relief, but I couldn't relax until we were far away from the deadly reach of Farmer Hudson's gun.

Tikky's back end was blocking the way out. "Get out of the way." I hissed. "What's the hold-up?"

Nel's silhouette in the open doorway assured me that Farmer Hudson hadn't come into the barn. I had no idea if he would, and I wasn't sticking around to find out. I turned to Lily. "Hurry up. Go on through. Shove Tikky out of the way if you have to."

"Mmph." She mumbled something I couldn't understand.

"Get going," I hissed.

Once the tip of her black tail disappeared through the hole, I slipped through and found myself face to face with Farmer Hudson's dog. Lily was on her back whining like a baby and Tikky was nowhere to be seen.

With my back to the wall and no place to go, I dug into the ground with my back feet and swiped my claws back and forth across Butch's nose.

He shook his head and snarled, "Quit that."

I couldn't stop myself. Frustration gushed out of me like water from an uncapped artesian wellspring. I slashed at his face and tore at his lip.

Lily, barking as if she had a sock stuffed in her mouth, ran in circles around us. From out of nowhere, Tikky leaped onto Butch's back.

Butch shook us off like we were nothing more than a few pesky mosquitoes. "I said stop that! You've got people." He gestured toward the front yard.

I had no idea if we were heading into the barrel of Farmer Hudson's gun, but it was the only way out.

Lily charged over us. I managed to pull a paw-full of hair from the tip of her tail when she bowled me over.

Chapter 30

Sage pulled the golf cart ...

...into Farmer Hudson's driveway.

She hopped out of the cart, ran up to the front door. and knocked.

The inside door opened. Farmer Hudson spoke through the screen.

"Morning Sage. It's been a busy day 'round here. What can I do for you?"

"Hi, Mr. Hudson. I'm looking for our pets. They haven't been home for two days. Ben and I looked for them all night last night."

"What kind of pets?"

"A black puppy and a black cat...."

"Got plenty of them in the barn." He stepped out onto the porch and leaned his shotgun against the door. "Seen one just a few minutes ago. A red one too. Butch is wandering around out there somewhere. He mighta' run them off. Ain't seen a puppy, though. I hope he don't come around here stealing my chickens like the one that just left."

"Our puppy is a female. Her name's Lily." Sage shook her head. "I'm sure she wouldn't do that."

"Yuh, that's what they all think, but critters is critters. They get hungry enough, they'll eat my chickens."

"Would it be all right if I looked in your barn? Maybe I'll find our cat."

Farmer Hudson picked up his gun. "Come ahead, take as many as you want. I got more cats than I need."

As they approached the open barn door, Lily charged headlong away from the protection of the barn. Tikky and I stopped at the corner of the building.

"Mwoomph, mwoomph."

What was wrong with Lily's barker? It sounded like the cat had her tongue.

"There she goes getting herself in trouble again," Tikky said.

"Mm hm." I kept my eye on the shotgun in between glances over my shoulder to see where Butch was.

"Lily!" Sage picked her up. "You silly."

Lily struggled, broke free, and headed back toward us. "Mwoomph. Mwoomph."

Peering around the corner of the barn, we watched her run toward us.

Behind her, Hudson lifted his gun and aimed. "Dog's got something in her mouth."

"What are you doing?" Sage pushed the barrel of the gun off Farmer Hudson's shoulder. "That's my dog." She ran to Lily. "Come here, now!" The Sage tone.

Lily stopped in front of us. "Mwoomph," she said.

"What's in your mouth?" I asked.

She dipped her head to the ground just as Sage grabbed her collar. "Lily!"

Sage saw us then. "Clawed! Oh my gosh, Tikky's here too." She scooped me up in her free arm. "Let's go. Come on, Tikky, if you want a ride.

"No thanks. See you later." He turned to leave. Butch glared at him. "Uh ... on second thought, here I come."

I'd always felt good in Sage's arms no matter how hard she held me while dragging Lily along.

We reached the golf cart. Sage pulled Lily up inside the golf cart. "Up on the seat." The Sage tone again. We all understood it. Sage didn't let go of Lily's collar.

She kept up a muffled whine all the way home. I sat squeezed between them. Tikky sat on the floor.

When we got home, Ben came out and grabbed Lily while Clawed and I jumped off the cart.

"Later," he said.

I nodded. "See you."

I followed Sage into the house. It was nice to be home. It didn't seem Lily thought so. She was spitting something out of her mouth, a white-greenish blob and lots of drool.

Sage rushed to her. "What's wrong, Lily? Aw, poor puppy. You all had a rough couple of days, didn't you?"

We sure had.

"You okay?"

"Woof. Woof!"

Sounded like Lily's barker was repaired.

"Good girl." Sage patted her and headed for the kitchen. We ran after her. "No treats right now." She waggled a finger in Lily's face. "I've got to clean up your mess."

"What about me?" I meowed.

Chapter 31

Tabbert, Tikky, and I sat on the cobbled path...

... taking in some rays. Tikky had learned how to climb the fence in and out. He was looking fit these days. I'm sure it had something to do with the bath Sage had given him and the bowl of food she left out regularly. Skeeter was resting on Tabbert's head. We were reviewing the events of recent days when Lily showed up. The leaves on the rose arbor no longer vibrated when she came through to Bling.

"I know, I know," Lily said when I reminded her she was not to dig in this area.

"Yeah, and no chasing lizards," Tabbert said.

I eyed him.

"Seriously, I thought she was going to eat me."

"I would never do that," Lily whined. "After Farmer Hudson shot at Clawed and Tikky and they ran into the barn, I found you on the floor." She shook her head. "I wasn't sure if you were dead or unconscious. Everything happened so quick. Tikky said we had to get going. Clawed was snapping at me to get going."

I hissed.

"Well, you were. I didn't want to hurt you with my teeth, so I licked you up. We jumped out between the loose boards, and there was Butch." She whined. "I almost swallowed you then. I ran as soon as Butch told us our people were here. I knew it had to be Sage and Ben. When I saw it was them, I came back to get you guys.

"Sage yanked me by the collar just as I was about to put Tabbert down. Seriously, you don't know how hard that was."

"Imagine how I felt. I'd already been shot!" Tabbert spun around and revealed the stubby end of what remained of his tail. "One of those BBs got me. Then you came along and gobbled me up. I thought I was a goner for sure.

"And here you are," I said. "So, stop worrying."

Tabbert crossed his arms and posed a defiant stance. "You're sticking up for the puppy now?"

"And you're letting a mosquito ride around on you."

Tabbert smiled. "Yup. She and I are practicing our act for the Blingling Fair. Watch." With Skeeter clinging to his head, Tabbert thrust out his dewlap, turned yellow, and completed several pushups.

Skeeter loop-de-looped into the air just as Tabbert spun in a circle. She did a figure 8 and a down loop-de-loop resting once again on Tabbert's shoulder. Their synchronization was perfect.

"Well done," I said. Feeling better than I had in months, I rolled over onto my back and let the sun warm my belly.

We had done it. All of us, not just me. We'd saved each other. Because that's what friends did. I had to accept that Gidget was....

Thinking of her reminded me of the last time I'd seen her and Stocker, the day I'd had a change of heart and went back to save Lily. They'd both said they were with me.

Hmph. We'd made it out on our own, without them.

"Really?"

I rolled over and jumped to my feet. Stocker and Gidget stood gazing up at me, side by side on the path.

"Who do you think managed Butch after you and Tikky practically assaulted him. Good thing I had Gidget with me. It took both of us to settle him down."

I settled down onto the warm cobblestones. "I believe you could have done it by yourself."

"Thank you for the vote of confidence, Clawed, but I've always found it's nice to have a little help from a friend."

I looked over at Tabbert, Skeeter, Tikky, and Lily. "Sure is."

When I glanced back, Gidget and Stocker were gone.

I sat back and looked up into a deep blue sky. "Did you see that?"

Tabbert came up beside me. "Sure did."

"What?" Lily stuck her nose into the blueberry flax. "What did you see?"

I headed back to the house with Tabbert clinging to my ear.

"You'll see. One day." Maybe I didn't like all dogs, but this one definitely was my new best friend.

The Rescue

While late to work alone I drove
and passed a misplaced blur.
It wasn't 'til a mile away
my brain told me 'twas fur.

I thought not of the consequence
and veered my car around.
I parked and stumbled in high heels
across the roadside ground.

A pair of eyes looked up in pain
and I beheld their plea.
They drew me in and stole my heart
and begged 'please rescue me'.

Some passers walking by in twos
came gathering round the pup
and cried with mortifying shock
when she failed to stand up.

Her struggles showed a mangled form
a mass of bleeding wound.
I could not leave her by the road
nor let it be her tomb.

My dignity does not allow
neglect of others' strife;
not even when the plight I faced
was simply one dog's life.

How could the world's best friend have known
that while she freely ran
her heedless antics as she played
would be hindered by man?

Dominion He gave us of things
from sea and land and air,
o'er cattle and o'er every
creeping thing that creepeth there.

And yet with buildings and paved roads
we block a Godly way
where eagles fly and whales swim deep
and puppies romp and play.

She only whined a little when
examined by a vet
"A sorry mess— she surely is,
but there's life in her yet."

He mended this and bandaged that;
stitched up her tattered skin.
Then while she convalesced, I prayed
if I should take her in.

Work filled my days, with family grown
my time held spacious gaps,
and I'd become an island in
a lonely sea, perhaps.

An answer quickly came to me.
A bold resounding voice
declared the deed already done
was clearly not my choice.

She came with me that very day

and settled in my home;
and ever since that one day passed
I have not felt alone.

The things that happen in our lives
are weighed down by much thought
But only God knows why he does
some things for lessons taught.

One mangled pup along the road
No longer running free
Now lives inside a fenced in yard
And, in fact, rescued me.

Other Books By Cindy Foley;

The Truth Lies…a Florida Saga
Water Drops
Chase A Dream Today
I, Clawed: The Renewal